KU-311-468

MEGAN NOLAN

Acts of
Desperation

CAVAN COUNTY LIBRARY

ACC No.

CLASS No.

INVOICE NO.

PRICE

VINTAGE

3 5 7 9 10 8 6 4

Vintage is part of the Penguin Random House group of companies
whose addresses can be found at global.penguinrandomhouse.com

Penguin
Random House
UK

Copyright © Megan Nolan 2021

The extract from 'Late Fragment' is from All of Us: The Collected Poems by
Raymond Carver, 1989, published by Harvill Secker. Reproduced by
permission of The Random House Group Ltd/Penguin Books Ltd ©,
Tess Gallagher and The Wylie Agency (UK) Ltd.

Megan Nolan has asserted her right to be identified as the
author of this Work in accordance with the Copyright,
Designs and Patents Act 1988

First published in Vintage in 2022
First published in hardback
by Jonathan Cape in 2021

penguin.co.uk/vintage

A CIP catalogue record for this book is
available from the British Library

ISBN 9781529113013 (B format)

Printed and bound in Great Britain by Clays Ltd, Elcograf S.p.A.

The authorised representative in the EEA is Penguin Random House Ireland,
Morrison Chambers, 32 Nassau Street, Dublin D02 YH68

Penguin Random House is committed to a sustainable future
for our business, our readers and our planet. This book is made
from Forest Stewardship Council® certified paper.

MIX
Paper from
responsible sources
FSC
www.fsc.org
FSC® C018179

CAVAN COUNTY LIBRARY
ACC No. 3455686
CLASS NO. F/IR
INVOICE NO. 11945 ILS
PRICE €6.68

For my mam, Sue, and my dad, Jim

Cavan County Library
Withdrawn Stock

And did you get what
you wanted from this life, even so?
I did.
And what did you want?
To call myself beloved, to feel myself
beloved on the earth.

Raymond Carver, 'Late Fragment'

A little girl of seventeen in a mental hospital told me she
was terrified because the Atom Bomb was inside her.

R.D. Laing, *The Divided Self*

April 2012
Dublin

CAVAN COUNTY
LIBRARY

1

The first time I saw him, I pitied him terribly.

I looked around to see where the drinks were, I was thirsty, and that's when it began.

He was standing in the gallery by a sculpture, a grotesque thing. It was pink and seemed to approximate some version of a mutated human ear.

He was deep in conversation with someone and gestured towards it vehemently as he spoke. I realised that it wasn't the first time I'd seen him.

I'd sat across from him once in the Rathmines Library and had been struck, then as now, by him being the most beautiful man I had ever seen. We had exchanged a long glance.

I had been with someone else then, and even if I hadn't, I had never approached a man in my life, not like that. I thought about him afterwards, and assumed he must have been passing through. Nobody who was like that, who looked like that, lived in Dublin, or Ireland, I thought. Nobody so beautiful could live with us.

Now he stood not ten feet away from me and I took him in again.

Ciaran was that downy, darkening blond of a baby just leaving its infancy.

He had large grey eyes, a crooked Roman nose, and a perfect cherubic mouth burning neatly beneath. The mouth was implausibly rosy and twisted a little, as though petulant, or always about to laugh. He was very tall and had the bad posture of someone who became so tall early and tried to hide it.

His hands were fine and disproportionately large, even taking into account the long limbs they were attached to. His bones seemed somehow more delicate than anyone else's. The features of his face were lovely too, but it was the way he was structured that made you lose your bearings first. The way his cheekbones were so high that they made his eyes cruel, the way his long fingers grasped purposefully at the air as he spoke, as though arranging decorations.

The thing to understand about Ciaran is not only that he was exceptionally beautiful, but that there was an immense stillness radiating from his body. The stillness was beneath every gesture, his glances, his laughs. He sought nothing from his surroundings.

In that kind of room, around art, where the person you are talking to is always looking over your shoulder for a curator, it was especially striking. Although he didn't seem particularly happy, he seemed undeniably whole, as though his world was contained within himself.

2

Is it possible to love someone without knowing them, by sight?

How can I describe what happened to me without the word love?

I stood in that gallery and felt not only sexual attraction (which I was aware of, dimly, as background noise) but what I can only describe as grave and troubling pity.

By this I don't mean that I felt myself to be above him. For almost our entire life together I would consider Ciaran to be better than me in both essential and superficial ways.

By pity, what I mean is that just by looking at him I felt an acute tenderness for his condition: his being human. In that moment the basic affection and sorrow I feel for any human person was intensified to such a degree I could not breathe.

Even now, even after all that took place between us, I still can feel how moved I am by him.

Ciaran was not the first beautiful man I slept with, or the first man I had obsessive feelings for, but he was the first man I worshipped. His body would become a site of prayer for me, a place where I could forget about my own living flesh and be only with his. It was a thing of total pleasure, total beauty.

Do you think I am unaware of calling his body a place, a thing? Do you think I am unaware of what it is to be a woman speaking this way about a man's body? What do I know about the body of a man – and can any single one of them deserve or need a moment more of praise?

What must it feel like to be beautiful but also invisible whenever you choose to be? To be a beautiful man?

3

Ciaran caught my eye, smiled slightly and widened his – in remembrance, I hoped, of our prior meeting. I walked towards him and he broke off from his conversation and turned to me.

'Ah, it's you,' he said, as though we had arranged to meet each other.

'The very same,' I said stupidly, and flushed with shame as I heard my voice as though from outside my head. It sounded very Irish and thick with forced joviality. Ciaran had an accent I couldn't place.

'What's your name?' I asked.

'Ciaran,' he said, and then, as though having read my mind, 'though it's only my father who's Irish – I'm Danish.'

I met his eyes then and my shame was overcome by the pleasure I could feel between us.

We smiled at each other shyly.

'What do you make of the show?'

'Oh, well,' I said, trying to answer as quickly and glibly as possible, 'it's just a bunch of things in a certain room, isn't it? It doesn't mean much to me. I come for the drinks.'

He ignored the last part of what I had said, which was intended to lead us out of where we were to some place more comfortable for me.

'Isn't it our job to try to understand: why these objects, in this particular room?' he asked.

I scanned his question for mockery, but he seemed to mean it innocently.

'It's just that with art I never feel on a sure footing. With other things, I have some knowledge I can discuss them in terms of. With this sort of thing, I could say anything at all about it. I have no frame of reference.'

He smiled at me again. There was something definitely sexual, almost gloating, in his eyes now.

'Well, that's just what I've always liked most about art.'

'Should we get a drink?' I asked.

'I'm leaving, and they're out anyway – here, have mine.' And he handed me his nearly full beer and picked up his bag. 'Would you like to come for a walk with me tomorrow?'

Taking my dopey gaze as agreement, he wrote his phone number on a napkin and gave it to me.

'Good,' he said, and was gone.

4

At that time I lived in a bedsit in Ranelagh on street level, where I left the window open at night so I could climb back in if I had lost my keys, which I often had. The first night I moved in, I sat in my bed after unpacking and looked around at the ephemera and trinkets. They were drawings and notes from old lovers and friends, postcards, photographs, porcelain figures, antique ashtrays. I needed these things, fixed them as soon as I arrived somewhere new, but now I was alone they seemed foolish. They looked like props for a bad theatre production, trying to summon up a personality where there was none.

Living alone, I began to split apart from myself in a deeper and more grotesque way than ever before.

There was my public life, where I worked and went out dancing and drinking and was amusing and energetic in company; where I made eyes at men in bars and sometimes went home with them; where I told people that I loved living alone, and they believed it because of how happy I was.

I really was happy when I seemed happy. I am incapable of lying about my feelings, it's only that the feelings have no coherence, are not continuous from one hour to the next.

And then there was the life I spent in my apartment trying to torture myself into submission and stillness. I could not be alone happily, and because I knew this was a sign of weakness, I forced myself to endure it for as long as I could before breaking, although I sometimes thought I would go mad.

Being with other people was, to me, the feeling of being realised. This was why I wanted to be in love. In love, you don't need the minute-to-minute physical presence of the beloved to realise you. Love itself sustains and validates the rotten moments you would otherwise be wasting while you practise being a person, pacing back and forth in your shitty apartment, holding off till seven to open the wine.

Being in love blesses you with a sort of grace. A friend once told me he imagined his father or God watching him while he works, to help force productivity. Being in love was like that to me, a shield, a higher purpose, a promise to something outside of yourself.

That night I first met Ciaran I got as drunk as I'd ever been. There were two kinds of drunk I could get. The first was generally solitary and born not of a desire to be drunk but to pass time less miserably. It was slow, perhaps a glass of wine every half an hour or so, not too immoderate, although never less than a bottle, and characterised by a maudlin self-pity that would sometimes sour into violence.

The other kind of drunk I got was far more excessive and characterised by exuberant good spirits and a communal edge of mania; on these nights I would spend a huge amount of money I did not have, because – even more so than usual – time beyond the present seemed absolutely unreal, and the needs of the present were urgent.

The excess of these nights was never depressing as it was happening, it was a part of being young and having no commitments and no stability. You could tell these nights before they had started usually, some air of mischief in the room when we began to drink. We threw back the first drinks, greedily anticipating the coming looseness and hysteria. There were things we had expected to have by now that we did not have.

Sometimes on nights like these I would meet people different to me, people who came from money and lived in flats their parents had given to them as casually as the rest of us were given charm bracelets and book tokens for birthdays. One such guy, Rogers, a small, wiry person with a great *Brideshead Revisited* pouffe of teased blond hair quivering above his porcelain face, dropped out of university about the same time as I had. I bumped into him at a party a few months later and asked what he was doing. I was surprised to learn he was in a middleweight role at a big PR firm, seeing as we were both only nineteen and without qualifications. I was still scrabbling around for miserably paid retail and bar work.

When I asked him, in all innocence, how he had pulled off such a thing, he winked at me and said, 'The Rogers name carries a lot of weight in this town!' This was a repellent enough statement to hear by itself, but became enjoyably absurd when a mutual friend disclosed that the firm was in fact owned by his parents. *The Rogers name carries a lot of weight in the Rogers family*, I thought to myself with moreish resentment each time I saw him from then on.

I, like most of my friends, was a good drunk, by which I mean I could drink a lot, liked to drink, and wasn't disagreeable once drunk.

My life was blighted by hangovers. I was hungover most mornings to some degree, and badly maybe twice a week. During bad ones, I missed whole days huddling in my bed, scrolling through my phone without pleasure or intent, locked into its repetition as a safeguard. I peered through the curtains at the 4 p.m. sun and thought it better to stay in until it got dark. I was badly afraid.

There was a questionnaire I took once to define one's level of alcohol dependence. The final question, in the section

11

that was supposed to mark out 'final-stage alcoholics near to death', was: 'Do you often wake up terribly frightened after a drinking binge?' And when I read that I thought, *Terribly frightened is exactly how I would put it.*

Terribly frightened. It summed up the somehow elderly sense of fear I had when I woke up in the mornings. It reminded me of cinematic depictions of old women teetering on the edge of dementia, whose husbands had died, and who couldn't remember the details of their home; an aimless but total distress and bewilderment. I woke up terribly frightened all the time.

William Faulkner, in the end stages of his alcoholism, travelled to New York to visit friends and see some plays. After ten days of heavy drinking he disappeared. A friend went to his hotel to check on him and, after banging on the door and yelling out his name to no avail, insisted that hotel staff let him in. Bursting into the room, they found Faulkner, semi-conscious and moaning thickly on the bathroom floor.

A curious, fetid odour hung in the air. The windows were all open despite the sub-zero temperatures. In the night, Faulkner had got up to be sick and had fallen against a radiator pipe. He immediately lost consciousness and did not feel the pipe burn through the flesh of his back over the course of many hours. By the time he was discovered the burn had become third degree.

In the hospital, his physician, Dr Joe, was called, and asked him, 'Why do you do it?'

Faulkner apparently jutted out his jaw and responded, 'Because I like to!'

His publisher Bennett went to be with him.

'Bill,' he said, and I imagine him looking down at his hands, head shaking slightly, unable to meet his friend's eyes, 'why would you do this on your vacation?'

Faulkner bristled at this, pulled himself up in the bed to his full height.

'Bennett,' he said, 'it was my vacation, after all.'

Why do you do it? Because I like to.

Meaning, not so much that I take pleasure in it, but: I choose it.

I do not understand what I do; for I don't do what I would like to do, but instead do what I hate. What an unhappy man I am. Who will rescue me from this body that is taking me to death?

–Romans 7:15–25

That night after meeting Ciaran I drank until I vomited and blood vessels beneath and above my eyes burst, and I traced them gently in the mirror, knowing they would be markers of a beginning.

5

Events that were objectively worse than what was to follow with Ciaran had taken place in my earlier adulthood, sordid checkpoints of the wounded woman. I cannot speak about these things too soon because their names alone summon like a charm the disinterest of an enlightened reader. Female suffering is cheap and is used cheaply by dishonest women who are looking only for attention – and of all our cardinal sins, seeking attention must surely be up there.

All the suffering I had so far endured before I met Ciaran, I had endured like a child. This is not to say the suffering was not severe, which it was, or that I did not understand it, which I did. But before Ciaran I still contemplated suffering as something with meaning. I understood even the most inexplicable of tragedies as being imbued with some as yet unknown purpose.

It was my feeling that there were lucky people and unlucky people, and I was a lucky person. Even in my worst depressions, I had always known this. My misery seemed to come from knowing I was not good enough to warrant the objectively lucky life I had been given.

I would not have thought so literally, or so religiously, as to say, 'Everything happens for a reason' or 'God doesn't give us more than we can bear', but the feeling was not so different. It was the feeling that each human life has a narrative and a destiny. It was the feeling that misfortune, no matter how great, would eventually serve to lead each of us to our own particular and inevitable conclusion.

My understanding was that every action would lead me to where I ought to be ultimately, and where I ought to be was in love.

Love was the great consolation, would set ablaze the fields of my life in one go, leaving nothing behind. I thought of it as the great leveller, as a force which would clean me and by its presence make me worthy of it. There was no religion in my life after early childhood, and a great faith in love was what I had cultivated instead.

Oh, don't laugh at me for this, for being a woman who says this to you. I hear myself speak.

15

6

I texted him in the morning and we agreed to meet at 2 p.m. outside the Natural History Museum. I showered in near-boiling water and spat blood into the sink when I brushed my teeth. I was badly hungover, but not ill, in the sweet spot before returning to full sobriety. I was glad to be so. Going through life hungover is an ordeal, but being without one is no picnic either. The fuzz and numbness of a hangover can carry you through a day without you noticing it too much; you're too busy tending to aches and thirsts to pay much attention to anything else that might trouble you.

I hadn't eaten since lunch the day before and was jittery as I walked. I tried to remember his face, and found that the intensity of my crush would not allow me to. I could recall individual parts but when I tried to assemble them they floated in a shimmering mess. I laughed at this nervously and shook my head, filled with affection for myself. I love myself in love. I find my feelings fascinating and human, for once can sympathise with my own actions.

When I arrived, he was drifting about the lawns looking at hedges sheared into animal shapes. I went to him and put my hand on his elbow, felt it warm in the worn old rust-coloured cardigan he wore. I had noticed this at the opening, too – he dressed in clothes that, although elegant on his body, looked on the point of collapse. They weren't merely distressed in a fashionable way but looked as though they had well and truly reached the end point of functioning as clothing. Instinctively I respected this: resourcefulness. My father told me once the trait he admires most in the world is resourcefulness, and since then I've looked out for it.

We hugged hello and I felt how slender he was beneath his soft worn layers. I sensed something slightly different from him than I had the night before. He was still powerfully calm, but there was a tension in his face. I wondered if he was nervous. My own nerves had mainly to do with the sobriety of what we were doing. All of my romantic affairs until then had begun while drunk, and most of them accidentally.

It was a bad location for a first date. We had to move around and focus our attention on things other than each other. We made observations about the exhibits between bouts of silence. We chatted enough to swap basic information in murmurs. I learned that he had moved permanently to Dublin a year ago, to spend time with his father who had become ill, but was doing better now. He had come from outside Copenhagen, where he wrote art criticism. Here he was trying to write his own essays, but his waged work was doing copy and reviews for a magazine.

The silences were making me unbearably anxious and I feared I would burst into laughter at any moment. Being in the museum wasn't helping; it was a shabby, dark and beautiful old place where the exhibits were sometimes unintentionally hilarious. My friends and I would go there hungover sometimes and become pleasantly hysterical at the old and incompetent taxidermy. But Ciaran was walking between them all in apparent seriousness, and I felt foolish for being amused.

I looked over at him for as long as I could get away with while he inspected the butterflies. I wanted to be nearer. I approached and held his worn elbow and asked if he'd like to go and get something to eat.

Outside, after walking down the staircase in more silence, he turned to me and said, 'Well. That was a very bad museum.' And his seriousness made me laugh then, and he laughed with me.

We spent the rest of the day together and spoke more about our lives. He described the town he was from and said he hadn't been sad to leave it. I told him about dropping out of university and the many odd jobs I had worked since then. I told him I wrote, too, in the way I always told people this: with the lowered pious eyes of a saint, looking away, worried and secretly a little hopeful they would want to ask me about it. This was not a justified worry when it came to most men and Ciaran was no different. He nodded briskly and moved the conversation on.

In the evening we walked along the quays and he left me to go and work in his studio. He kissed me, and then held my head in his hands, studying my face with fond satisfaction, and said we would see each other soon.

As we walked in opposite directions, I turned back to look at him over my shoulder and he did the same to me and I was filled with a soaring levity. We were both laughing, and I turned away from him and started to run – had to, the feeling was so strong. I ran and ran and I couldn't stop laughing in amazement, thinking of how he kissed me, thinking that there was nobody else I wanted to kiss now.

When I look back, what I find most odd was how sedate the day with him had been. We had got along fine, had found each other agreeable, were obviously attracted to one another, but there was no moment of breakthrough in the conversation. The moment I had shared with others before him, when you feel all the pieces lining up as a rhythm takes hold, had not occurred.

18

I think even then in that first flush, running up the quays alongside the April sunset, I was aware of that. It didn't matter to me how funny he was, or what he thought of me, or what books we had both read.

I was in love with him from the beginning, and there wasn't a thing he or anybody else could do to change it.

7

Before Ciaran I tried some other men on for size. I was trying a lot of things. I had become a strange age. I was no longer the barely-legal-but-knowing teenager who had wielded such power over men. Nor was I anything like a self-possessed adult woman who might attract them by way of her autonomy.

People enjoyed me, because while I was attractive enough I was not intimidating. I was buoyant and good-natured and occasionally a little bit mean in an amusing way. I looked and fucked like a woman but could drink and take drugs and talk like a lad. I would bring some effete long-limbed DJ home with me and in the morning we could knock about town together without the awkward suggestion of romance or obligation.

We could have coffee, in our farcical fur coats, or a conspiratorial too-early beer, before going our separate ways, and then I would see them that same night at another club, with one of the girls who was more like a real girl to them, girls who were tall and willowy and part-time modelling while they studied fine art. I think that I wanted more than anything to be real like those girls, but I didn't know how to be, didn't know any other way to be close to these boys except for partying with them. I was not without value, but the value I held was not the kind I wanted to hold, and I did not know how to exchange it.

My life as a party girl dwindled away. I slept with too many people's boyfriends, got sick in too many front rooms. I stopped being enjoyably fun and became only frantically fun, and then felt too old for it all anyway.

I fell into the habit of being only with much older men. Not knowing what to do with myself, it was simple to stumble into their lives. Whether I was truly beautiful, exceptional, interesting mattered less with them. I was still very young in the grand scheme of things, if not young enough to be a nightlife novelty any longer. I was young enough to be compelling to them by virtue only of my youth, standing in as a monument to whatever things they felt they no longer had access to.

I met one such man at a book launch not long before I would meet Ciaran. He was an editor at a small independent poetry press, American. He wore funny thick glasses and sweater vests and had a honking, obliviously loud speaking voice, which was what made me notice him first. He was talking to a friend throughout the book launch's tedious speeches, with so little care for his surroundings that it made me laugh. His friend replied in whispers and tried to shush him but the editor didn't seem to notice and went on broadcasting his flat Californian drawl. He caught my eye and grinned at me, and we drank together for the rest of the night.

It was sort of amazing seeing men who weren't particularly attractive but who believed, more or less correctly, that they could have and do whatever they wanted. I was always calculating with scientific precision the relative beauty of the people I wanted to be with, and would steer clear of the ones who exceeded me too greatly. But then you'd see guys like this one trundling around the world, reaching out, cheerily thoughtless, for whatever shiny thing

21

passed. They didn't feel the need to strike an equitable bargain, they just advanced towards you, grinning a little sheepishly maybe, and their entitlement was so alien and enviable that it was something like charming.

'I have a sort of girlfriend,' he gasped into my mouth after he had pushed me against a wall.

'Okay,' I said in response, then rolled my eyes and kissed him again.

When he took me to his house for the first time some weeks later I immediately lost the upper hand it had felt as though I had. He was rich. It was a huge two-bedroom apartment in Merrion Square, everything in soft-brushed fabrics and beige tones. A small sleepy corgi named Dots blinked up at us from the sofa. Being young and beautiful felt like a lot sometimes, felt like it translated to real-world power, but money shat all over it every time.

He took me to bed, where I was uncharacteristically shy. The grandeur of the house felt oppressive, my cheap high-street lingerie crude. Eventually he undressed me fully and laid me out on the bed, kneeling over me and patiently removing my hands each time they returned to protect my most embarrassing parts. He did this until I stopped trying to cover myself and lay there still beneath his gaze. He looked so happy, taking me in. He touched each part of me, and kissed my forehead gently.

'I've wanted this for a long time,' he said. 'Since I first saw you.'

'Me too,' I said back, but I knew that I didn't mean it. I hadn't wanted to sleep with him. I had wanted never to sleep with him, had wanted us to keep talking, to wake up to his messages, to be amused by one another. I wanted our chaste coffee dates to go on and on, for there to be no end to these things, and this, the sex, was the end, I knew.

It felt good in a way, because he was so excited and I was pleased to make him so, but I was filled with sadness at each new thing he did to me. Every thing he did was another ending. When we had done all the things there were to do, he passed out and I clung to his reassuringly solid, soft stomach – paternal, so different to the indie waifs – and cried.

In the morning I woke up before him and went to the kitchen for water. I walked around and noticed things I had been too drunk to the night before. One room was wall-to-wall books, so comforting and stable to stand beneath. There were armchairs in different corners, where two people could sit reading in happy silence all day long before reintroducing themselves when evening came and it was time to be together again. I petted Dots, who panted happily, and looked out the window into the square and imagined what it would be like to walk her there every morning and every night, a routine so regular as that, a life where you knew what to do when you woke up.

I went back into the bedroom and noticed a pair of high heels and a bottle of perfume and some Avène moisturiser in a corner on the side of bed I had been sleeping in. His girlfriend, I thought, could be my mother's age. Here was an actual life, a real life, which I had walked into, dragging the mud of myself with me. I had never felt so unlike a human being, so disposable and flimsy and built purely for function. He called me a cab to go home and I knew I would never hear from him again and I never did.

8

I was waitressing in a hipster burger restaurant then, skittish from the running around and the bumps of coke we did in the toilets on double shifts. My friend Lisa and I lived together in a house we called the Ski Cabin for its weird low wooden ceilings and the feeling you got that they were going to slowly envelop you. Lisa and I met our very first week in Dublin, both sulking anxiously at the fringes of some nightmarish freshers' week event, locking eyes in anguished relief. She was from a town considered even more small-time and hokey than my own by the confident Dublin people, who considered everyone from outside of their own hopelessly provincial suburbs to be 'culchies', farmers, inbred and unsophisticated.

We were close straight away and remained so even after I dropped out of college abruptly. When she said she wanted to go out dancing, I was surprised to find that she meant it literally and not as a euphemism for getting drunk. Though I drank much more than she did, I appreciated that she never made me feel self-conscious about it, or even gave the sense that she would notice such a thing. She was wide eyed and gregarious and rarely alone. There seemed to be no part of her that wished for anonymity or the privacy of solitude. I admired this in her, the ease of it and the goodness, knowing as I did the different texture of my own solicitation of company, which was conditional and explosive when not satisfied.

We moved in together when she had graduated and were both waitressing full time or as near to it as the whims of our managers allowed. We spent our days off huddled in blankets and fleeces on our awful bony couch, listening to the radio and writing in our notebooks or sending emails or 'doing research', which for me meant reading the Wikipedias of lesser-known serial killers and jotting down the details that struck me: 'While holding the girl hostage, he gave his victim the book *Treasure Island* to read and watched the movie *Hook* with her.' Or, 'The killer could achieve sexual release as an adolescent only when he cut holes in photographs of women.'

We drank strong tea with the teabags left in and chain-smoked roll-up cigarettes, and sometimes when the day had passed we would work on a crossword together. We cooked meals of tinned pulses and wilted greens with lots of garlic, chopped tomatoes and anchovies. We cracked an egg into more or less everything and let it cook and set off the stove, mopping it all up with leftover bread one of us had taken home from the restaurants we worked in. Though I was restless in a way Lisa never was, waiting anxiously for what was to come next, I felt soothed by our domestic union. I admired the way she had of making any place into a home – within days of our arriving, even the appalling damp toilet had wall hangings and figurines and felt ours.

She was so wholesome that I sometimes didn't know how to react to her except by rolling my eyes, as though her picnics and sober dinner parties with edible flowers and whole roasted fish and adventures on trains were an affront to me. In fact, I wanted to want them, would have loved to live a life like that. Or rather I would have loved to *appear* to live a life like that. All the things that Lisa did for her own genuine pleasure were things I thought looked good, things I didn't want for their own sake. I thought a life that looked that way – clean and gentle and high-minded – would get me what I truly wanted, which was to do with having as much of people as possible, their attention, their desire, their curiosity.

Sometimes I thought about people like Lisa – people who never lost control of themselves, who never had too much of anything, who were never awake after one a.m. – with something like disdain. I valued what I thought of as my free nature, my willingness to do whatever I wanted at all times, my ability to be led by whatever base physical urge was singing to me in each moment. Wasn't there some truth to the way I existed that those safer people were too timid to follow in their own lives? It didn't occur to me that maybe Lisa was doing exactly what she wanted to do, that what she wanted was to live in the calm and benevolent way that she did. I didn't think so because it was incomprehensible to me that someone could drink and lack the desire to keep on drinking, I didn't understand that some people didn't have that want inside them.

She sat down some evenings and opened a bottle of red one of us had stolen from our restaurants, and took a little sip, and then a bigger one, and exhaled with pleasure and set it down and drank it over the course of an hour or two as she read or busied herself in the kitchen. Enjoying the first glass of wine was an alien idea to me, I who drained them within a quick grimace, alcohol tasting foul and acidic on top of the permanent hangover until the first two took effect.

On my twenty-first birthday I had a party in our house. Lisa and her new girlfriend Hen baked me a cake in the kitchen. I heard their excitable fresh-romance conversation thrumming sweetly below as I got ready in my room, and they cooed as I descended the Ski Cabin's spiral staircase in my sweeping red dress.

Lisa had done the thing that seemed as impossible as moderate drinking to me: she had remained single – actually single rather than single-and-dating – until she found someone right for her. She had barely kissed anyone in the time I had known her and I wondered privately how she wasn't bored or lonely, but I knew too that this was the better way to live. You earned the eventual love story with your restraint.

So it happened for Lisa, she made her own life, one that was happy and fully formed. Then Hen arrived into it and that was that. They were in love and there was nothing torturous or humiliating about it. It was as they said it would be, and I knew that it could never happen that way for me because I couldn't spend a day, much less a series of years, without looking around me for someone to feel things about.

I remember that a lot of people complimented the drama of my birthday dress, and invited me to twirl around so they could see it splay out around me in its red cloud, and that I felt beautiful and funny. I remember everyone leaving to go to a bar at some point, and that I had an altercation with a neighbour of ours after we trundled out and lingered on the pavement smoking and waiting for the others. I remember Lisa's arm on mine as I was rude to the neighbour, defiant in my birthday glamour. Then I remember nothing at all until I awoke the next afternoon, inexplicably in Lisa's bed rather than my own.

I climbed carefully down the stairs, depth perception shot, and saw Lisa cleaning up pizza boxes and cans overflowing with ash.

'Agh, what happened last night?' I said, trying to sound casual, a laugh in my voice, stomach tense with fright. 'Why was I in your bed?'

'You bled in yours last night and wandered out, so I put you in my bed after I cleaned up.'

She was tidying and wouldn't look up and meet my eye.

'Oh my God, I'm so sorry, Lisa. I must have taken out my tampon when I was drunk or something. Jesus, I'm really sorry.'

'You were in there with Peter,' she said, frowning at this having been the case and at her having to tell me so.

Peter was the on/off boyfriend of a good mutual friend of Lisa's and mine, a sweet girl called Greta who was looked upon with patronising compassion by everyone who knew her for being unaware of Peter's philandering.

I didn't know what to say, so instead I laughed shrilly and said, again, 'Oh my God!', as though what she had said was just an ordinary embarrassment like spilling a drink. Then she did look up at me and what destroyed me was that, overriding her disdain for what I had done, there was such troubled concern. In that moment I knew that Lisa, and only Lisa, was able to see me as I really was. She alone could see the reservoirs of need that existed in me and would never stop spilling out, ruining all they touched, and she didn't hate me for them, but felt sorry for me. This appalling and instant knowledge cut into me and I recoiled, turning from her and returning upstairs until I heard her leave the house.

It wasn't long after the party that Lisa told me she was moving to Berlin with Hen. A part of me was relieved. I couldn't stand to live with her any longer after the way she had looked at me that morning, but nor could I bear for her to drop me. I didn't want her near me, because she was the only one able to see me for what I was, but I couldn't lose her for the very same reason.

I made sure to spend the months before she left being a faithful and devoted friend. I was trying to say without words that I needed her, of all the things I needed, she was the only one that was good, and I would need her even more after she left me. She promised that she would not stop being my friend just because she was moving, and was mostly as good as her word.

9

Ciaran and I saw each other a few times a week after our first date. Most often I would finish a late shift in the restaurant and walk or get a taxi to go and stay in his apartment. He lived in a ground-floor flat near the jail in Kilmainham. He didn't mind the hours I kept. He never slept well and would only ever pass out fitfully between 4 and 8 or so. I arrived still gently sweating and smelling of the kitchen. He ran me a bath and I lay in it for a while, listening to him hum and make us tea or hot chocolate and put some stale biscuits on a saucer.

He didn't drink much and didn't care at all about food. He had lost his sense of smell and most of his taste in a car accident in infancy, and never had anything but what he needed to fuel himself – great reserves of bland muesli, tins of chickpeas, white rice. After I drained the bath he passed me a T-shirt and old waffle fabric long johns of his, which were soft from age and filled with holes. Although I slept over frequently I never brought my own things to sleep in. I liked the feeling of his clothes close to my skin and smelling his Pears soap smell.

Then we would sit on his couch hugging and touching each other slowly, speaking quietly about our days. We were so kind those evenings. Laughing softly, indulgently, at the other's little observations. We touched each other with such care and delicacy, as though afraid to break the new thing we were to one another.

When we had sex for the first time I felt out of my mind with happiness, with the obvious rightness of what was happening between us. Around his mouth there was some perfect smell that I could almost taste – I knew whatever made up that indefinable smell was also in the chemicals that drove our bodies together.

(A few weeks later in work, one of the chefs made a truffle-essence. He passed it to me, saying, 'Smell that!' I waved it under my nose and thought instantly, *It's Ciaran.*)

We listened to records most evenings. He liked Bob Dylan and Hank Williams and so I did, too. Sometimes we would rent films and watch them in his bed. He was so big I could sit cradled in his lap without causing him discomfort. We watched schlocky 50s B-movies, which we both liked but he found especially hilarious. I was always curious to see what he would find funny or what would make him happy. He was so solemn.

In the beginning it seemed like the solemnity of a toddler learning their surroundings; an innocent or even admirable one, a necessary impulse caused by new information. Perhaps he was like this because of being new to Dublin, I thought. But as we came to know each other better I began to see the other side of this solemnity.

He was angry at a great many things, disgusted by more. He didn't understand events which seemed completely normal, if not ideal, to me. When we took walks in Merrion Square or in Phoenix Park on Sundays, children on the street sometimes shouted insults after him because of his glasses or his shabby clothes. He grew incandescent with rage. 'Why are they like this?' he demanded of me, looking back over his shoulder as though wanting to start an argument with them. I would try to steer him on as gently as I could, sympathising and agreeing.

Our conversations in his apartment could veer into thirty-minute rants about a homeless person on the street who had offended him in some way, or an artist he had run into who was rude to him. He would eventually stand up, furiously rolling his cigarette, then pace around smoking as he recounted the perceived slight. His anger was always contained enough that it didn't alarm me, and in fact there was something invigorating about him venting his grievances to me, something unifying and bonding.

I would offer comically exaggerated sympathy, tug at his tattered sleeve as he walked to and fro and pull him towards me on the couch. 'Oh, poor baby,' I'd crow, and cradle his head to my chest and cover his face in a flood of kisses until I succeeded in making him laugh.

10

At the end of May I asked Ciaran to come with me to a reading at a gallery some friends of mine were doing. He had met some of them before, in passing, or had known them slightly from openings. This was the first time we were arriving together to an event and behaving as a couple publicly. To my mind, we spent so much time together already that we functionally were a couple, whether or not we were named as such.

Ciaran was tetchy and stony-faced from the beginning. He hadn't wanted to come, but had already arranged to see me that evening, and had no good reason to cancel. As we stood around chatting to people, he said nothing, and gazed over our heads as though disturbed by some presence invisible to the rest of us.

I caught several people exchanging quick glances that seemed to note his strange behaviour. I had seen him be quiet in company before, but never completely rude. I was embarrassed, and talked louder and faster to compensate. I held his hand gently, and when the conversation arrived at a publication he sometimes worked for, I turned and directed a question to him. He nodded very slightly and continued to look away, dropping his hand out of mine and putting it in his pocket.

During the readings his face was fixed in an almost comically extreme expression of disdain. I kept my eyes forward and hoped nobody else would notice. Once it was over I took him by the sleeve and dragged him outside so we wouldn't get trapped talking to anyone else.

'What are you doing?' he said, shaking me off.

'Why are you being so rude?'

I hated myself for being near tears, but I was. I had been looking forward to going there with him, introducing him to people, being seen with my beautiful, interesting boyfriend.

'That reading was shit.'

He shook his head, fumbling for tobacco in his bag. Glancing up at me, he saw that I was going to cry. He clocked the tears and caught my eye, jutting his jaw and pursing his mouth in an exaggerated gesture of disgust that I would come to know very well and hate completely.

'Of course it was shit!' I said. 'It's just a stupid reading. It's what you do, you go to things your friends do to be supportive, and you pretend they're good even if they're not.'

'These people aren't my friends. Just because you and I sleep together, it doesn't make them my friends.'

I didn't know how to respond to this. 'Sleeping together' was the least generous reading of what had been going on between us and could only have been intended to hurt me. I lowered my head and let myself cry, aware of people I knew looking at me from the gallery porch and whispering to each other.

'What?' he said. 'Did you want me to say I'm falling in love with you? Because I'm not.'

'No,' I said, and feeling that I had no more energy to do whatever we were doing, I turned and walked towards home.

11

It was the first time he had been cold in this way to me, although I had glimpsed his coldness before.

One evening in his kitchen we had been talking about the performance artist Chris Burden, who I knew of for having allowed himself to be shot in the shoulder for a film. Ciaran's eyes lit up, and he said I ought to read about *TV Hijack*. He grabbed his phone and showed me a picture of a man standing behind a woman in a chair with his hand pressed to her throat. The backdrop was bright blue. She seemed to be struggling to escape the man's grip.

Ciaran explained. This was one of Burden's earlier works, born from his interest in television, more famously illustrated in his later work, *TV Ads*. The circumstances that led to *Hijack* were this: an art critic named Phyllis Lutjeans had asked Burden to do a piece on an arts and culture show she presented on local television. Several proposals Burden made were rejected by the station or Lutjeans, and he agreed instead to do an interview. He insisted that the interview be broadcast live.

When he arrived, Lutjeans began by asking him to talk about some of the actions he had proposed which were ultimately shut down. At this point, Burden stood behind her and held a knife to her throat. He threatened to kill her if the station stopped broadcasting. He then went on to detail what he had wanted to do, which was to force her to perform obscene acts live on air.

Lutjeans was unaware of Burden's plans. Her alarm and humiliation were real.

I listened as Ciaran talked, and stared at the picture with growing unease.

'She didn't know?' I asked. 'He just pulled a knife on her?'

'That's beside the point,' he said. 'Anyway, she didn't mind. She said so later.'

Reading about her afterwards, I found interviews in which she confirmed she was not complicit, was shocked and frightened, but defended the piece – it was simply Burden's style.

I thought about this, about what the alternative was. I thought about Lutjeans being released from Burden's grip and spinning to face him, searching his face, the second in which she had to decide whether to cry and scream at him, or to wink.

What would you choose? Either you can be famous for being a shrill prop in a great man's work, a victim sacrificed to the gods of art, or you can nod along and applaud. You can have a seat at the big boys' table for being such a good sport. So, go ahead: ha ha ha.

2019, Athens

Mediating your own victimhood is just part of being a woman. Using it or denying it, hating it or loving it, and all of these at once. Being a victim is boring for everyone involved. It is boring for me to present myself through experiences which are instrumentalised constantly as narrative devices in soap operas and tabloids.

Is this why I am so ashamed of talking about certain events, or of finding them interesting? This is part of the horror of being hurt generically. Your experiences are so common that they become impossible to speak about in an interesting way.

If I want to say something about my hurt, I hear my voice enter the canon of Women Who've Been Hurt, becoming unknown, not-mine.

I can't, and don't much want, to make myself understood. Why should I make my experience particular, and what would be the point? Should I tell you about rape?

I was angry at having been made real in that way against my will. There is good reason for not living inside your body all the time, and this event trapped me back in it for a long while, until I could struggle back outside again.

The functionality of it depressed me, that I was so prosaic. My body was not glorious or miraculous or alive, it was just a thing of use. This did not sadden or surprise, so much as bore me: I looked at myself, lumpen and inelegant and abused, and thought: So what?

The act of unwanted sex was not what angered me most, but rather the tedious reminder that men can often do whatever they want and that some of them will. I know it is unfashionable to describe rape as sex (the implication being that rape is a violent, rather than a sexual act; can't it be both? And sometimes more one than the other?) but it felt very much like sex to me. From a purely physical point of view it didn't even feel very different to some of the worse consensual sex I had had, those times where I had realised immediately that I would rather not continue, but did so to be polite, feigning enjoyment to make it end quicker.

It would be easier if I could paint a line down the middle of the house, and have rape on one side and sex on the other. I have had sex without wanting to many times in my life. It was only once that I protested and was over-powered.

I feel no common understanding grow between myself and other women who have been hurt in the same ways that I have, no thread of sisterhood connecting our experiences. The inherent tenderness of the person (me) who is raped, their assumed softness, pliancy disgusts me – the femaleness of that disgusts me.

Am I ashamed of myself for this? Of course; somewhat; a little.

12

A few days after our fight at the reading, Ciaran called and asked to come over. Convinced he was going to break up with me, I sat up waiting for his knock. When he arrived he was wet-eyed and soft like I'd never seen him.

We sat side by side, not touching, for a long time. I was bursting to say I had been an idiot, that I wanted him to forget the whole evening, couldn't we just go back to how we had been, whatever that was? Couldn't we – please, please, please?

Before I could launch into this he began to speak. As always when he spoke about anything personal he seemed physically strained and could not look up, but he struggled through what he had prepared.

He was sorry.

He needed me to understand that what had happened between him and Freja, his ex, had scarred him. She had been unfaithful to him, not just with one man, but with many men, not in isolated instances but constantly throughout their long relationship. She had been the first woman he loved, and when he found out about her betrayals they had entered into a long period of vicious arguments, followed by tearful reunions, late-night screaming followed by going out and drinking and vengefully fucking strangers.

They had been bound up in each other so inextricably he didn't think they could ever get away from each other. It was only when his father became ill and he decided to move to Ireland that he realised they had a chance to make a clean break.

'You have to understand,' he said, 'the best times of my life were with Freja. She is not a bad person.'

I narrowed my eyes.

'She did terrible things,' he said, 'but they were really because she was unhappy. It hurt her that she did them to me. I hate her, but I also love her. Can you understand?'

My mind was working double-time to selectively absorb and reject the various things he was telling me. He was sorry: good. He was opening up about his past: good. He loved her: bad.

'Yes,' I said, trying to be mature.

'It hurt me so much that, since then, I haven't wanted to be close to anyone. I was exhausted. I don't want to be hurt any more, or hurt anyone else. But I want to try. I don't want to hurt you,' he said, and in that moment I remember thinking, clear as a bell, that I could never hurt him. I remember the fierceness in my chest. I promised myself I would make him trust me. I would rebuild what she had taken away from him.

He pressed his burning forehead to mine and we closed our eyes and were together.

November 2012

1

I separated my life with Ciaran from my life with my friends. I would still bring him to things occasionally, but only big public events which would not require us to stay too long or to talk to people. Although he was rarely again so rude as he had been at the reading where we had our first argument, he was not good at faking enjoyment.

Eventually it seemed easiest to let him do what pleased him, and see my friends on my own time. That he and they disliked each other was sometimes inconvenient, but no more than that. I preferred to be with Ciaran on my own anyway.

He was sullen and angry less frequently now. When he complained, he did so with some self-deprecation and conceded that he was behaving like a cantankerous old man. It had become cold and he wore a battered old pea coat and fingerless gloves and a thin ineffectual tartan scarf. I don't remember a single argument in that part of the year. I was moving through our relationship with concentrated deter-mination. With every week that passed, I felt safer and more at ease with him; the passing time legitimised the relationship and I was especially happy every time a new month began.

We met in April, I thought, and now it's November. We had passed two whole seasons together and were making good headway on the next.

2

It was two a.m. one weekend evening. We had just finished having sex and I had gone to his kitchen to get us some water, and as I settled back into bed he asked, 'How many people have you slept with?'

'Why?' I replied, keeping my voice neutral and low.

'I was talking about it with someone at work recently and it became an interesting conversation. I just wondered.'

I thought of Freja cheating on him with multiple men. I did some quick calculations: how many boyfriends I had mentioned to him, who else I might have alluded to, what was a reasonable lie.

'Nine,' I said.

'You see?' he said, very quickly, sitting up and turning to me like he was expecting it. 'I've slept with nine people too, and you're years younger than me. Everyone I know has slept with more people than me. What is it with people? Do they just do it with anyone?'

I didn't know how many people I'd slept with. It was probably something like thirty then, maybe more. I had lost substantial chunks of time to drink when I first left home, couldn't and didn't want to remember exactly what had happened.

It wasn't the lie that disturbed me, but how quickly I knew how to do it.

3

During this time I drank less, and only seriously with my friends. Ciaran was grossed out by drunk people and said that he didn't like to do it much himself, but on weekends sometimes we'd stand outside The Stag's Head and he would get tipsy after two or three pints.

I loved him to be drunk. I loved us drunk together. He was not a good drunk in the sense that I was, tipping along more or less the same as ever – he was a great drunk. His seriousness evaporated, and he was excitable and funny. His eyes glazed over with bleary fondness and he was as sloppily affectionate as a kid, grabbing me and whirling me round and dipping me and covering me with kisses. He was happy, which he never was for very long when sober. Of course, it was a false happiness, but when it was so easily and frequently accessed who could blame me for believing in it?

On a Saturday night we might, at my demand, have White Russians and watch horror films and listen to records until dawn. That was even better – when it was just us he would sometimes let go, drink until he was really drunk, and we would dance around the living room, laughing and laughing.

I pinned him down on the couch and tickled him and pressed my mouth to that amazing place between belly button and belt buckle and he would shriek and squirm. We fell together on to the ground, tactile and giddy. We fucked there on the ratty old carpet on nights like these, flushed and breathless from our wrestling. In the morning I would get a fright from some violent inflamed bruises on my knees or back and then realise with a smile it was from this.

It was the beginning of one such evening that the incident about his poems for Freja took place.

We were drinking at a bar near his place, a sort of faux-dive with neon lettering and sawdust on the floor. We were sitting at the bar on swivel stools, facing in towards each other, hands on the other's legs, or idling at the neck, or brushing the lips, always touching somewhere.

We were talking about Ciaran's writing. He was now in a comfortable enough position he could take an extra day off a week to focus on his own creative work. He had never allowed me to read anything he had written except reviews and academic writing, most of which was meaningless to me. He was talking about a series of poems he had started on. I was nodding along, feeling proud and supportive, when something slipped through the veil of drunkenness.

'… and that chapter will include the poems I've been writing about Freja …'

Freja's name had rarely come up since our conversation about her six months previously. This had been fine with me. I was so determined and sure that things were going to be perfect between Ciaran and me that I didn't have room for her.

'What poems?' I asked, heart pounding.

'I must have mentioned it before,' he said, taking a slug of his beer. 'No? I've been writing a series about her and our relationship, especially the early part when we lived in Oslo together.'

46

I nodded slowly, taking this in, sized it up as quick as I could.

Don't make a big deal of this, I told myself. I was pragmatic, entering panic mode already, trying to recover my composure.

(What could people be expected to tolerate of me? How much of what I needed could I reasonably demand?)

(Nothing, nothing, nothing.)

I went to the bathroom and stood in front of the sink and wept bitterly, immediately, without thought. I knew it was childish, behaving this way, but it was painful to be reminded so casually that everything I cared about was subject to the whims of others.

I walked back out and sat on the stool, touched his face, squeezed his knee, smiled as best I could. He looked bashful, but was grinning dopily too. I thought to myself, with the smallest hint of distaste, that he wouldn't have told me if he wasn't drunk. For all his performative distaste towards sloppy drunks, he could be one too.

'You're not upset, are you?'

'No, of course not. Just surprised.'

'Good, good.' He was still smiling that vague, idiotic smile, not really looking at me directly.

'Because I think, actually, they're quite good. Freja was impressed.'

My face crumpled involuntarily, as it had privately at the sink a few moments before.

'You sent them to her? You sent Freja poems you wrote for her?'

'To get her opinion, yes. And I thought she'd like to see them. We're just friends, you know.'

I stared at him, disbelieving, overcome. I didn't cry really, only there was some physical breakdown, which I could feel and which must have been visible.

I hadn't known until that moment how delicately I had been keeping everything inside me together those last few months. My body felt as though it had been holding its breath for a very long time and had just realised it couldn't do so for ever.

What I was feeling was the failure of superstition and charms – the unreliability of prayer.

4

When I was a child and my cat was hit by a speeding car that didn't stop, he lay out in the shed that night waiting to be buried.

I crept out into the damp mossy darkness after everyone was asleep and drew back the blanket he was beneath. I put my hand on his familiar ginger stomach but of course it was wrong in every conceivable way: freezing where it should have been warm, stiff as new cardboard where it should have been soft.

Feeling this wrongness I knew it was true at last, and couldn't believe it. I kept on stroking and stroking him, making deals with God. Thinking, *If I stand here all night*; thinking maybe if I stroked the awful, dead-thing stomach one thousand times exactly, thinking, *Please, please, God, send him back to me, give him back to me, I won't stop asking*.

5

I had been living in a constant bargain with Ciaran for months. Every day that passed in which I was easy to be with, and accommodating, and a good girlfriend, was a ritual offered up. My body expected the perseverance to mean something. And suddenly it was clear that my intentions were meaningless, and I could no more magic him into loving me than I could an animal back to life.

When I looked back at him from my collapse, he had hardened.

'For God's sake. Don't be a child.'

There was a scrape as he pushed his stool back and moved past me.

'Wait,' my mouth was saying instinctively.

I wish I could step inside this memory and steady myself, put a cool reassuring hand on my own and convince myself to wait. Have another drink, calm down, go home. But my body was moving without thought, scurrying under the bar to gather my belongings, running outside on to the tram tracks, peering in both directions. I saw him walking quickly down past the National Museum. He was moving steadily, betraying no sign of the drunkenness from a moment before. I ran after him, feebly calling wait, wait, and grasped for his shoulder when I caught up to him.

He shook me off so violently that I stumbled backwards, and then I was crying and saying please over and over again.

Ciaran found crying repulsive. Whatever distaste he already felt for me during arguments, the sight of tears sharpened it. His eyes would narrow and lose any residual warmth or compassion. He would turn away from me, refuse to witness.

Was he right to be disgusted? Was it all a show, a ploy to get sympathy? I can only say if it was one, it was both unconscious and misguided. It never succeeded in eliciting any good or compassionate feeling, and yet I kept doing it. I never wanted to. It seemed as impossible to restrain as vomit, and its ability to repel him only made me do it harder.

It was, I think, that loss of control he hated above all. To see an adult really cry is a perverse experience. The wailing adult is both childlike and pathetically defeated in a way that is alien to childhood (cursed by the breadth of their experience, lacking the single-minded purity of a child's grief).

Some part of me had already decided to live for him and let him take over the great weight of myself. I was also so frightened of him and what he did to me that I could never admit this decision, inwardly or to him.

And so in moments like this one when I was unexpectedly confronted by my own need, my reaction was to deny – to hysterically deny – that it existed. Hence the wailing of sorrys and pleases, the desire to make him forget at once I had ever demanded anything of him.

In these moments – for this was only the first of what amounted eventually to hundreds, whole months, years, of prostrating – I pleaded with him to see how small I really was.

I said through my huddling and hiding that I was nothing, and I was happy to be nothing if nothing was what pleased him best. If nothing was the least trouble, then I would be it, and gladly. I would be completely blank and still if that was what worked, or as loud as he needed me to be to take up his silences. I would be energetic and lively if he was bored, and when he tired of that, I would become as prosaic and dully useful as cutlery.

I didn't ask love of him. I didn't want him to look in my direction and see me; for there was no thing I could say, with confidence, was me. I panicked when my need shone through because it was real.

The need was a true and human part of me, but I could feel nothing else of myself to be true or human, and so the need seemed ungodly, an aberration.

He walked home and did not actively discourage me from following him. He ignored me, which I could tolerate, in that moment even enjoyed, the better to demonstrate how quiet and good I could be. When we reached his house he stopped outside and turned to me.

'You can come in, and you can stay, but I do not want to talk about this tonight or ever again. Freja and I are adults. We're older than you. We have a complicated relationship, but it has nothing to do with you and it does not affect you. Understand?'

I nodded eagerly. I didn't speak again that evening, brushing my teeth and undressing in silence. I allowed him to turn away from me in the bed, as I knew he would, without protest.

I woke at dawn. Outside, the sky was a bright and sterile grey. Christmas wasn't long away.

I looked down at Ciaran, frowning in his sleep. He seemed so young when he slept, his skinniness more apparent in the tight old T-shirt he wore. The damp heat he radiated was that of a child sweating out a fever. It is still especially easy for me to love him when I think of him this way. He seemed somehow pre-historic, still-becoming, an animal not yet ready to exist, with whom there is no point in being disappointed.

I crawled out of bed carefully, my stomach a pit of nausea and dread. I walked out into the front room and stared out the window, stretching and reaching towards the ceiling.

I glanced around and thought about eating some muesli when I saw Ciaran's phone lying on the table. The sums were done in seconds. He was in the deeper part of his sleep; I would hear him getting up; his phone didn't have a lock key.

I knew I was entering new territory from which I couldn't return. I was invading him and his privacy, just as I had tried so hard to imply that I wouldn't with my submission.

I opened his email account. Almost all of the emails were to and from Freja. I scrolled down. They had spoken nearly every day for months, the entire time I had known him.

I opened the most recent one she had sent, shortly before I had met him in the bar the day before. I skimmed it quickly, not daring to take enough time to read it all. It was long, a few thousand words. The first few paragraphs were a critical response to the poems he had sent, and then she began to talk about me.

'...Now, having read your poems, it's my turn to impose on you. I try to talk to you about us and you stop me by mentioning her. We both know you use her to get at me and make me jealous. There is no need. You've succeeded. I am jealous. I'm miserable. I'm angry. I think about the two of you all the time, idle away hours in the office finding pictures of her online, trying to imagine what you see in her.

'She's cute I can see, but a little chubby for you, no? You used to like that I was long and thin, not at all like her. Is that it? That she is so unlike me? Am I so terrible that you are cursed to seek my opposite? Doesn't it feel strange to be in bed with her and not me, after all these years?

'Do people ever tell you and her that you make a beautiful couple, like they used to with us? We looked right together because we are right together. Do you remember the first night in the new house in Oslo after we moved everything in and unpacked? Once we were done we sat on the porch drinking whiskies and looking around us at our new home, and an old lady walked past and stopped. She looked at us and said, "Aren't you two the most beautiful couple I've ever seen," and we laughed and she said, "Be good to one another" as she walked off. She could see how in love we were even at that distance, because everyone could.

'When we met, we were both lost and hopeless. That's part of why we love each other. I saw it in you from the beginning. There was a broken part in us both that only the other could mend, that's why we had to be together. I woke up every day back then with you staring down at me, stroking my hair, as though you couldn't believe I was real. You can't take back or deny what exists between us.

'Remember those days we would walk for hours in Nordmarka until we could barely take another step, then go home and take a bath together. You read your poems to me or we talked about what I was reading in school, and we dried each other off and fell asleep on the couch in front of the fire.

'Do you expect me to believe you have what we had with her? I know you. I know what's inside of you, and how little you can show it to people.

'If only you would give us another chance, I could prove it to you. Besides, what I did was only ever sex. It meant nothing. I never did what you are doing now. I never played house with anyone else, went on dates or any of that shit.

'You left here because of your father, but he's fine now. You say yourself you never see him. Come back to me. Or I'll come there – I don't care. I would go anywhere.

'I don't exist without you. When I come home after work I put on your old sweater and put it to my face,

54

trying to gather any remaining scent. I think about kissing your collarbone, your ribs, your eyelids. I close my eyes and imagine the feeling of you coming back to me, of us disappearing together.

'You know me, Ciaran. I don't have boyfriends. Before you there were only people I had slept with. I've never loved anyone but you, and I have loved you for so long now. Seven years. This isn't like other relationships. I'm not going to get over it and move on to the next one. It's only you.

'It will only ever be you.'

Crazy bitch, crazy bitch, I thought. Horrified jealousy was pulsing through my body like poison. *Crazy bitch, crazy bitch.*

I was sickened by her over-familiarity, her wheedling self-pity, the linguistic melodrama, but mostly by the smug portrayal of what they'd been like as a couple. Reading poems in the bath, chuckling about what a beautiful pair they were, some mutual understanding that they were more troubled than anyone else.

I heard a rustling in the bedroom and quickly exited his email and shut the phone back off. I ran the tap and filled a glass with water and went back to the bedroom. I slid in beside Ciaran, my chin on his shoulder, hugging him from behind. He cast his arm backwards and held me to him.

2019, Athens

Being in love feels like nothing so much as hope; a distilled, clear hope which would be impossible to manufacture on your own.

One of the saddest things to feel is that nothing in the world is new, that you have exhausted all your interactions with it. When I feel that way I wake each day into the already-dusky afternoon with deep regret that nothing has happened overnight to change me. I wake so late because although I can't stand to be conscious, I can't stand to try to sleep either. To lie down in the dark and think, for even a moment, seems an unspeakable prospect, so I drink until I pass out, or stare at the television until my eyes physically can't stay open any longer.

If I try to travel my way out of this feeling, cities blur into one another. I waste money feeling bad in a piazza by myself, twelve-euro bland pasta, too much wine, some dull man always trying to speak with me.

When I go home to Waterford to try to even out and reconnect with myself and my past, people seem to be dying all the time all around me, and I argue with my parents about my reluctance to engage with them. I don't want to hear about the illnesses and tragedies, and am amazed by their ability to keep attending funeral after funeral. It feels as though all I can do each day is eat and sleep and trudge through the hours and start again – and, in fact, it is all I can do. Anti-depressants come and go, making little difference either way to the fact that my reaction to all of life, all of God's green earth, all of mankind, is often: So?

And then, whenever I fall in love, everything is made new, including myself. My body, my brain, the way I see the simplest things. And the best part is it doesn't even have to be the first time to work. If I fuck it up once, the next time works just as well.

Looking out windows on public transport becomes unbearably stimulating, fields of rapeseed bringing tears to my eyes, the jagged coastline taking my breath away. My mind, which had seemed so stagnant and grey, feels suddenly like a baby's, absorbent and crackling with new information. The new person not only makes a depressing and boring life feel interesting, but makes it into an entirely different kind of life. Afternoons, which I might otherwise spend cowering alone in bed hiding from errant sunlight coming through the curtain, I now might spend feeding ducks and reading poetry by the canal. A transformation which is the nearest to actual magic I have ever come.

When you fall in love with someone and your life is remade, you know instinctively that you must take great care of this delicate new world the two of you are building. There is infrastructure to be dealt with, dams and bridges and town halls to be planned. The high-stakes precarity of what you are doing will frequently bring tears to your eyes, both from fright and from exquisite pleasure. One wrong move and the whole thing could collapse before you have even finished construction. Couples will often disappear together for months in their beginning stages, which is not just about lust but also about building.

6

When Ciaran and I went to the cinema in our first few weeks I remember wishing I could watch a film of him, even while he sat there beside me holding my hand. I remember wanting a screen so big that I could see nothing outside of it. I wanted to be totally saturated by him, for there to be no room for anything else to leak in. I knew I was about to begin the most difficult and important building of my life. I felt on the cusp of a grand project, my best work yet. I would build a great sturdy red barn which could stand for centuries. I would build a magnificent golden cathedral. I would build the eighth wonder of the world.

When I read Freja's email to him, my mind could not understand it in terms of my project, and so I couldn't fully absorb it. The idea of our newly built world not continuing to exist was literally inconceivable to me. It was easy to deny because trouble receded when I could be with him physically, all potential intrusions rendered laughably unreal.

I had sex with him that dawn and was totally free of disquiet. To feel his long, strong fingers wrapped lightly around my throat. The smell around his mouth, the sweetness, hovering over mine. I arched my back up to get closer, tried to inhale that breath. I raised my hand to his jaw and held it still so that he was looking right into my eyes as he moved, and doing that made each individual second sacred.

Just as, in my younger days, my partying had seemed somehow important – seemed somehow to be getting at something bigger than other people were able to get at by doing the same thing – sex with Ciaran seemed *important*. It seemed each time to be driving towards a conclusion, and the conclusion would teach us something profound, if we ever arrived to it.

7

Things were good between us for the next few weeks, better than before, as though something foul had been released. I thought about the email, but with disgusted anger towards her only, nothing towards him.

I was shocked by the totality of the world she had described in her letter. The particular intimacy of her tone in addressing him, the details I would never have had cause to know if I hadn't read it.

I tried to imagine the sweater of his she had kept, the porch they sat on, what view they had from it. It was disturbing, as it always was to be made aware that people with their own internal lives and individual perspectives existed all around you.

The idea of her having a long-held perception of who Ciaran was, which predated mine by years, was awful, but its otherness was also erotic. For the first time I googled her, to see what she looked like. At night sometimes when I couldn't sleep my mind would force me to imagine them fucking.

Ciaran was gentler with me than before, and sweeter. He bought me little things and surprised me with flowers and took me out for dinner.

These things seemed especially significant to me since he was mean with money. He didn't make a lot, but nor did I, nor did anyone I knew. If I didn't have change on me to get a coffee he would pay for it but would always, always ask for it back. I found this bizarre and uncomfortable.

It wasn't just with me. I'd seen him claim back drinks owed to him by friends who had no idea what he was talking about. When they'd turn their heads quizzically he'd recite the exact scene:

'Don't you remember, Harry, it was in the Duke after the second-to-last IMMA party? It was the week before your payday so I got you a beer.'

And everyone would laugh and roll their eyes about his stinginess. I found it harder to laugh, found it more genuinely embarrassing, because I was his girlfriend. I feared vaguely that this meanness implied other things to people, that they were embarrassed on my behalf.

Once, after a bunch of us had gone to dinner in a sushi place after an opening on Talbot Street, he had almost pushed a girl to tears. She was an intern at a gallery in town, new to Dublin, just moved over from Krakow and she clearly had a huge crush on Ciaran. She was younger than me, nineteen or so, with a lot of clean shiny hair and big solicitous eyes. She stared at him all night.

This happened all the time. Usually I didn't mind much because he never noticed. It was a strange experience for me to be going out with someone so objectively attractive. In public, I was split between taking childish pleasure in it and feeling terrified that people looked at us and were puzzled by the discrepancy.

At the end of the dinner, Ciaran was settling up the bill and telling everyone what they owed. The intern was a few euro short.

'It's fifteen,' he kept repeating. 'That's what you spent, with the beer.'

'I'm sorry, I … I …'

He laughed, as though in disbelief. 'I just don't understand why you would order fifteen euros' worth of food and beer if you don't have it.'

Our end of the table had turned to look.

'Here, I've got it,' said her boss at the gallery, leaning across to toss a note in and giving Ciaran a funny glance.

He took me out on the last night I was in town before Christmas. We went to a French restaurant and ate rare steak and drank expensive red wine. He was nice to the waiter and ordered for us both in a way that made me feel small and contained and happy. We talked about bad shows we had seen and laughed about the artists and their ladder-climbing desperation, their sad trucker caps and hip tracksuits they were too old to pull off.

His lips were a little stained from the wine and he seemed incredibly sexy to me as we spoke, completely open and alive, none of his usual reserve or irritation interrupted us. When we were leaving, I pushed my chair back from the table and he stepped behind to help me put on my coat and dipped down to kiss me. I thought of everyone in the restaurant seeing us like this, as we truly were, as we would be from now on – two young, interesting, beautiful people at the beginning of life together. I glanced around as we left, at the other couples – and I was right, people really were looking.

A pair of older women smiled indulgently at us as we passed them. The female half of an expensively dressed and meticulously groomed couple stared at us with an expression I couldn't identify. I was flushed, head swimming with pride. We were something real, whatever problems we had were unimportant, were only a consequence of how intense it was to really live.

He walked me down to Eden Quay, and we stood in the shadow of the bank buildings which lined that side of the river. He held my hands in his and kissed my ears and blew warm breath on them. As the bus pulled up, he took a small, pale blue box out of his bag and handed it to me.

'There's your present,' he said, and bent down, rubbing the side of his soft cheek against mine like a cat, kissing my forehead. 'I love you.'

A profound calm swept over my body, affirmation that I was not crazy. We looked at one another, kissed again, laughed at our serious faces, and hugged a last time.

I climbed on to the bus and found a seat as far as possible from anyone else. I wanted to be alone and catalogue all the feelings I was experiencing, examine them one by one. I couldn't help myself from opening the box. Inside was a folded-over scrap of paper on which he had written:

Happy Christmas. You are a beautiful woman and I love you.

Beneath the note was a delicate antique amber brooch. I held the stone in my hand and squeezed my eyes shut. It seemed to radiate heat, to throb, like a living thing. I was still holding it when we reached Waterford three hours later and the approaching lights of my home city made me cry as they did every time I arrived upon them.

2019, Athens

I was sitting in a café last week, reading my book and drinking a coffee before catching a train. It was a clear evening, the sun had just set, when an enormous electrical storm descended without warning. The waiters moved us all further inside the patio under a larger awning to avoid being splashed. Me, a businesswoman in her fifties and a couple of indifferent old men sat there looking out at it. The businesswoman was wearing a lot of very red lipstick and kept raising her hand to her mouth in fright when the lightning appeared. I was watching her and it with half-interest when a young couple with a baby in a pram ran in.

They were very beautiful and very wet and they were laughing. The woman was doubled up, clutching her stomach, howling with it, and her husband put his hand on her shoulder and rubbed her back affectionately. They looked around at the rest of us, with these big incredulous smiles on their faces. Look, their smiles seemed to say, at the rain! Look how wet we have become! Even after they had settled at a table and lifted their baby on to their laps, they kept breaking down into shuddering laughter every few moments.

I felt so lonely when I looked at them, remembering (but not quite clearly; through a veil) what they were experiencing; that part of being in love that makes inane experiences valuable. Laughing at getting rained on instead of it just being a minor pain on your way somewhere else. And even after, when they were just sitting eating sandwiches and drinking coffee, their contentment was amazing to see. I had forgotten that love has the power to do that. I envied them, felt glad for them, and frightened for myself. Having a sandwich and a cup of coffee in the rain was nothing I could render magical by myself.

It reminded me of when Ciaran would wake me in the mornings sometimes and ask what we should do that day. I would say, 'Mm, I don't know, we could see a film in the evening, or go to a gallery.' And he would say, 'Or, let's just get apples and walk around.'

And this became a thing we did together, a thing I would get excited to get out of bed to do. We would walk into town and go to the fancy supermarket café on George's Street and drink a couple of glasses of their tap water by the counter as the waiter looked on annoyed. Then we would buy (or sometimes shoplift if we were after an illicit thrill) two apples. We'd spend a few minutes picking them out, comparing them, weighing up size relative to flavour. Then we'd leave and for four or five hours we would walk around the city, just talking to each other and seeing what was going on. We certainly could stop into a gallery, or a charity shop, or to get a coffee somewhere along the way, but it wasn't the point.

Getting apples and walking around was the point, just that, that was the whole point. That was more than enough.

Christmas 2012
Waterford

1

When the bus pulled in it was almost three a.m. and I was a few miles from my mother's house.

She had lived in the suburb, Ballinakill Downs, since she and my father separated when I was small. Her second husband, Stíofán, moved in eight years later as I was turning fourteen. Mam's name was Keelin until she met Stíofán, who was a school teacher and gaelgóir, and then she abandoned the anglicised version for the properly Irish 'Caoilfhaoinn', and snapped at you if you pronounced it the old way.

An objective outsider would think Mam had been the winner in the contest of their divorce, her tall rugged new husband, the kayaking trips and weekends away, but privately I thought that Dad was the happier of the two. I worried over his loneliness, but he was an easily pleased man, in need of not much more than a degree of casual company, reading material, and a bit of land. All of these he had in his small village a few miles outside the city, where he worked in their hokey library and drank with the same three pals a few times a week.

Mam seemed always to be anticipating disaster in a way that seemed unnatural and pointless for a person in their later life, and still anxiously dieted with the vehemence and optimism of a teenager.

'How's Stephen?' my dad would ask her whenever she dropped me off to his house, where I spent most of my weekends, throwing me a wink.

'It's Stíofán, as you well know, *Tomás*,' she'd say back to Dad, who had only ever been called Thomas.

Usually when I came home from Dublin at that hour I would have called a taxi, too lazy and afraid to walk to Ballinakill, but now I could think of nothing more wonderful. I listened to music that reminded me of him on my way, and felt a quiet dreaminess I hadn't since I was a teenager. When I got home I let myself in and Mam was sleeping on the couch with a crime drama on TV.

'Hi, child,' she said, one eye opening.

'Hi, mother,' I replied, going over to squeeze her hand hello, before going up to bed.

I slept for twelve hours straight, as I often did when I first came home, as though recovering from having to be alive on my own all year round. When I woke, although it was only 19 December, my bedroom had the feeling of Christmas already. I reached down for my bag and took out the amber brooch and held it in my hand, feeling it warm.

That day and the next I sat in our living room and read fat silly novels of the sort I didn't allow myself normally, helped to wrap presents, cooked. I drank wine with my mother and gossiped about people we knew and watched bad television. On the night of the 21st, I called Ciaran, not having heard from him since I left. I wasn't alarmed – he was useless with his phone and rarely had credit unless I bought it for him. After three tries, he hadn't answered. I was tipsy and eager to talk with him, but didn't think much of it. I topped up his phone online and sent him a message saying to call me when he was free and that I missed and loved him. It felt cheering to write it down.

On the 23rd I went for drinks with two old friends of mine. On my walk to meet them I caught a glimpse of myself in a shop window and had to stop and steady myself against a post. I was so disgusting. I was so big. When I got to the pub, people would talk about it, would stare and whisper about how much bigger and uglier I was than when I was younger.

I felt my stomach against the elastic of my underwear, spilling over it, both me and monstrously not-me. That I wasn't thin was not the only thing about me, a fact which seemed obvious everywhere else in the world. But when I returned to Waterford it seemed again my defining trait, my characteristic failure. Every time I came back it was a reminder that, at least there, at least home, at least where it counted, I would always be wrong. I would always look like a misshapen version of my True Self, a hastily sketched approximation of a human being.

2019, Athens

I've never understood how people can love their bodies, nor really understood how they can hate them either. I've always seen my body as nothing so much as deeply disturbing in its constant variance, a fluctuating, unmanageable thing that has basically nothing to do with me, is not really any of my business at all.

How am I supposed to accept or like or hate or be neutral about a thing that will not stay the same? How can I maintain consistent feelings towards a changing thing like that? Should I concede instead that I can't, that it's necessary instead to cleave my body – in all its hideous wilful growth and recession and blooming and withering – from myself, from me?

I am told this is impossible. I am told this most often by men. They have studied philosophers I haven't, but the things they say in dressed-up terms are just like the florid self-help slogans by women they think are stupid. The things they say are: You are your body. There is no divide. When it changes, that's you changing. You are not just a witness to your body's vagaries, you are the architect.

People are scared of teenagers having sex but we might think sometimes about the misery of having a teenage body, a teenage girl's body especially, how tedious and painful and punitive, and remember that sex might be the first time she realises that bodies can be made to feel good. That the

72

million sensitive places which cause you to feel pain can also be sensitive to pleasure. That when you want to cry it will not always be from sadness.

My body disgusted me when I was that age, but at the same time I was learning to love it – love it too much. I hated it but also worshipped it with an obscene devotion, because I knew what it was capable of inciting in myself and in others. In the mirror, I wanted to cry out with distress one moment, wanted to break the glass and cut great chunks of it away. The next I was on my knees staring in dizzy adoration, grazing my hands over the gentle shelving of my ribs, looking down at it from the same angle a boy would. I was on my back in bed with a camera, I was reflecting on how lucky anyone would be to see a sight like this.

There is no truce to be made with my body; if I make one, I know it will only be negated by a new enemy in time. What is the point?

When I go back home I am angrier than ever. I am all at once submerged in every body I ever was, all the failed attempts at being a certain kind of person. My old scales are there, my old photographs, the skin across my face taut with hunger, my eyes bright and wild with it, very beautiful, nobody could deny.

And at home there is my mother. Around her I am ever more nauseated by myself. There are the usual itemised wrongs in my head, the ones I might trot out to a therapist, throwaway comments she made when I was at formative ages. She was always somewhat mad about her own body, but especially when she was young and single and probably driven to distraction with a whiny child and little idea of what the rest of her life might look like, if it would be any good.

She said these things without any meanness or vitriol, said them in the same chipper conversational way she said most everything, but of course I remember them. So unfair – I'm sure I don't remember hundreds, thousands of other things she said, telling me I was fine as I was. It seems likely. But nevertheless, I don't remember them, they don't exist for me.

Instead, what exists are the moments like this one: I was eleven and the usual routine was for my mother to collect me after school, and on the drive home we would stop and get me a snack from the shop, a packet of crisps or a cereal bar. This particular afternoon I had decided I was going to become skinny and virtuous like the healthy trim little girls in my class who ate rice cakes and whose socks did not strain against their calves in the least.

'What do you want to eat?' my mother asked.

'Nothing,' I said, 'I'm just going to have chewing gum after school from now on.'

'Good girl,' she said, and I remember feeling a sad, deep worry that she had been hating me all along for the eating I was doing before, that she had been waiting for me to give it up.

When I come home now, still, I am self-conscious and defensive before her. I hate that she can see what weight I have gained. I hate to listen to what she is or isn't eating any more, what she is doing at the gym. I hate that hearing those things feels like a dare to me, or an invitation to raise the stakes. I hate that I have never found an appropriate response, that all I can do is defensively eat nothing, in a rage, or eat everything, showing her that I am past that, I have transcended her petty concerns, I am mind, not body, I am better than her. I stop wearing the kinds of clothes I wear in my normal life, fun and pretty ones, and recede into sullen, voluminous sweatshirts.

Even if my mother had never uttered a word about her body or mine, I think I would still feel this way when I come home, the same claustrophobic fury under that shared roof, the two of us so close together. I came from her, she made this body-thing I hate and love so much. I resent her for producing it; I'm mortified I have made such poor use of it. How dare you? I want to scream at her, on the one hand; I love you so much! I'm sorry, on the other.

2

By the morning of the 24th, Ciaran still hadn't called and I was veering into dread. I tried to comfort myself – maybe he had lost his phone. Then why was it still on? Maybe he was just busy. Too busy to send a text in four days? We hadn't spent so long without talking in months. I began to genuinely worry – he didn't have close friends who would be checking in on him, he wasn't due to see anyone until Christmas Day. He refused to spend any of the holiday with his father in Wicklow, claiming that the usual mutual grumpiness which existed between them soured into outright aggression whenever he had tried to, that there were resentments from childhood Christmases which would not stop resurfacing no matter how much time passed. Instead, he had dinner with friends on the day itself and visited his father in January, when the worst of the feeling had passed.

Maybe he had had an accident? He could have fallen while cycling, or just slipped coming out of the shower and hit his head, or – or anything.

A few hours before I was to meet my dad for a walk, I called Ciaran's office. I knew he wouldn't be there: his holidays began the day before. His boss Michael, who I knew socially from openings, answered the phone.

'Hi, Michael,' I said, trying to sound casual. 'Sorry to bother you – I'm just wondering if Ciaran was in yesterday.

I've broken my phone and I don't know his number off so I haven't been able to get hold of him.'

'Happy Christmas! Lucky you, you've been down the country all week, haven't you? I'm nearly finished now but I'm the only one left here who can do layout for January so … anyway! Yeah, Ciaran, he was here until lunchtime or so, I told him to go home then. He was fidgeting so much all he was doing was annoying me, ha. I've got his mobile here somewhere; I can give it to you if that's any use?'

'Ah!' I heard myself say with a forced laugh. 'That would be great.'

He read out the number, and I repeated it back as though I was writing it down, as though I didn't already know.

I called him constantly for the rest of the morning, knowing there would be no answer, but unable to stop myself. The frenzied certainty that a terrible thing had taken place was stronger now, but no longer was the terrible thing a cracked skull or a blocked windpipe. The terrible thing was a mystery now. I could focus only on the immediate. I needed with every part of my body for him to pick up the phone. That was the only thing I could think of; the sound of his voice saying hello. Everything after that would be dealt with.

My dad picked me up at lunchtime and we went for coffee and a walk. I struggled to appear relaxed and happy. I answered his questions about Ciaran as brightly and truthfully as possible. Because of our closeness he knew I was lying about something, and having ascertained I wouldn't be telling him what it was, became brisk with worry and frustration.

I wished I could unburden myself but I couldn't verbalise what was happening because doing so would bring it into existence. So far, it was all taking place in my head with no verification from an outside party, and so long as I kept it that way I could suppress it. That urge you have with an envelope of results, delaying the future in which you are unwillingly privy to terrible news.

I knew also that if I began to describe more or less anything about Ciaran and what our relationship was like I would upset my dad. The split in me was so wide that these two states could coexist:

1. I knew that my relationship was strange and uneven and not reciprocal and that speaking about its reality would confuse and upset people who loved me.
2. I didn't feel it to be those things.

That is, I could understand that a truthful account of it, according to actual events, would sound disturbing, but I did not feel disturbed by it. It was only that other people would be incapable of understanding the way in which objective reality did not account for its essential truth.

I could not withhold from my dad as easily as I could with others. When I obscured or omitted important things, I couldn't then behave normally. Usually when I did this it was to avoid upsetting him, when the problem was something he could not help with and I could therefore see no point in burdening him.

It had been like this when I was a teenager. My depressions were without source or resolution, and so I had no real answer to the question 'What's wrong?' My relationship with Ciaran had the same feeling of inevitability. It just was. I just was in love with him, and any of the problems that came with it were simply to be borne. There was no point in describing them.

The denial of information to Dad made me feel weak and depressed at the irreconcilable distance between us, which was so much smaller than between most people, but still existed and always would.

Sometimes this distance between everyone comforted and pleased me. I would die knowing things about myself that nobody else on earth did. There were experiences that lived only in me and could never be replicated or recounted. And sometimes, like now, the distance seemed too sad to live with.

In the car on the way home we were chatting idly about his eldest brother leaving home when he was a kid, and I asked if his parents had minded him going away.

'Same as me with you, I suppose,' he said. 'I'd prefer if you were here for my own sake but I wouldn't wish it on you. The thing that gets at me sometimes, like now getting to spend a relatively long time, more than a day, is thinking about how little this will happen again.'

'What do you mean?' I asked.

'I mean, if you count the times we'll spend a significant amount of time together from now on, more than a day at a time ... those stints are limited. They're very limited, really.'

He was driving, frowning slightly out the windscreen at the winter sun, and didn't seem distressed by what he was saying, had said it matter-of-factly.

I turned my face to the side and stared out my window. I was filled not only with misery about what he was saying, and his awareness of it, but also with shame at how squalidly I was wasting my short life. I was sitting in a car with someone who loved me more than life itself, and yet all I could think about was Ciaran. How impoverished my internal life had become, the scrabbling for a token of love from somebody who didn't want to offer it.

3

On Christmas morning I woke up at seven and sent a message to him:

> *Happy Christmas. I love you very much. Please call me.*

I irritated myself as I wrote it, the 'very much' shrill and manipulative.

I ate breakfast nervously and exchanged gifts with my mam and Stíofán and then Dad collected me. We drove to meet my grandmother and uncles at the church we always went to for Christmas. We looked for them when we got in, but the service was beginning so we slipped into the nearest pew. In front of us an elderly woman was crying silently into her hands, an adult son sat beside her with his arm firmly around her shoulder. *Her husband must have died*, I thought, imagining it, *and this is the first Christmas without him*.

Then I was off too – the combination of witnessing her grief, standing there with my father, being in the church I had come to in my school days. I hardly let up for the next thirty minutes, breaking down utterly hearing my dad's strong tuneless voice join in with 'Silent Night'.

I said sorry to my dad afterwards, but he understood. He suffers too.

We went to the graveyard to do our traditional walk to see his own father's stone, and that of my mother's mother. In the car we avoided each other's eyes and spoke with wobbling voices, and as we arrived back at Mam's house he put his hand on my wrist and said, 'It'll be OK,' and I was sad for him that he had had a child at all if it meant his happiness was tied to mine always. I was sad I wasn't able to learn to be happier, more regular and peaceful, because it meant he would never have that peace for himself, which he of all people deserved and had waited for.

It was painful that he loved me so much and wanted things for me I knew I would never have and never deserve. I owed him so much and I would never repay it. I wished I could somehow make him understand this so he could give up on me. I kissed him on the cheek and said, 'I know, Dad. Love you, I'll ring you from Dublin,' and left the car quickly before we could hurt each other any more.

The rest of the day was easier. I drank wine on the couch and read and smiled listening to my aunties teasing Mam as she cooked the dinner and felt happy in the complete containment of the house, and wished I could stay in it for ever, wished I could erase all the other parts of my life and give up on the idea of progress. We ate and played board games and drank and smoked and watched films and at the end of the night I went on to my mam's couch and curled up next to her and cried and cried and she petted my hair and didn't make me say what was wrong. The next morning I left before anyone was awake and got the bus back to Dublin.

4

The city was still quiet and empty when we pulled into it just after nine. I walked home, crossing over O'Connell Bridge slowly so as not to slip on the ice. I went up Grafton Street where people were gathering for the sales, stopped for a coffee at the top and went around the edge of Stephen's Green, where I often walked with Ciaran after work. I was putting off the moment of unlocking my door and stepping in to the emptiness and having whatever was happening happen to me.

I was often like this on evenings when I wasn't seeing Ciaran after work. I'd begin the walk up and be filled with lurching dread at the thought of all the steps yet to take, the familiar corners to turn, the nothing, the nobody, waiting for me when I got there. I'd stop into a pub on the way, buy a magazine, anxiously smoke and sip two glasses of red wine and pick at my hands until I forced myself to leave.

It was like that now but worse. It took me an hour and a half to do the forty-minute walk, wandering in wrong directions and stopping to look at shop window displays. I unlocked the door and sat on my bed, unpacking the few things from home. I took out the note: *You are a beautiful woman and I love you*. Looking at it agitated me further. How could he have written it if – he can't have written this and then –

I put it away and took out my phone and messaged him that I was home and I was going to come to his house. He replied immediately: *Stay there I'll be there in an hour.*

I clung to the phone, flooding with relief.

There had to be some explanation for what was taking place. His dad could be ill – could be in the house with him, for all I knew.

I made coffee and smoked and tapped the kitchen table, looked at the note. Stroked my hands, soothing myself, trying not to bite them or hurt myself.

He knocked on the door exactly an hour later. When I opened it, he had changed entirely. The momentary hardness that crossed his face during arguments was total now, and occupied every part of him.

'Come in,' I said.

'No,' he said.

'What?' And losing it already, all of the pent-up energy of useless hope draining in a moment, my body sagging, I grabbed the doorframe to stay upright.

'I'm not coming in.' I looked again at his face, it cut into me. 'I came here to tell you it's over. I'm leaving now.'

And he really did turn to leave.

How did he do it? It was amazing, remarkable to me even through the sickening shock of it; how could a person be the way he was?

'Wait, please, come back,' I heard myself say, hating the sound of my craziness, and calculating quickly what would make him come back. 'Five minutes, I swear, just five minutes.'

He turned back and stood as he had before, with one hand on his backpack strap and one on his hip. A stance of parental irritation, one you might take with a child who won't stop asking why they can't have ice cream for dinner.

And indeed, he was narrowing his eyes, shaking his head, as though I was asking an impossibly grandiose favour of him. His expression suggested that whatever was taking place was a usual thing that I was failing to understand because I was stupid, or unwilling, or delusional.

'Why?' I asked. 'Please come in and talk to me. You have to talk to me. Talk to me.'

My voice was raising with each sentence as he shook his head at me.

I searched, trying to push through like there was some telekinesis fuelled by desperation and love I could use to penetrate him.

'I'm not coming in,' he said again, and in the madness of the moment I was in, this was the only thing to overcome. It was like my feeling that hearing him pick up the phone would resolve everything when he had disappeared. If I could just get him over the threshold, get him to step into my normal, same old room – if I could get him to sit on the bed we had slept and loved each other in, he would surely relent.

He would have to break his surreal character, would be forced to remember and soften.

'Please come in and talk to me,' I begged, and with a petulant sigh he came through the door and threw down his bag.

'What?' he said.

I didn't know where to start, how to describe the lunacy of what was taking place between us, what to demand of him first. The nearest thing I had to evidence was the proximity of our last meeting. I grabbed my bag and scrabbled for the blue box. I held out the amber to him as though it was a talisman, as though it could summon something from within him.

'You gave me this, you told me you loved me, a week ago!'

I was screaming now and along with everything else I hated him for making me into this.

I felt crushed with the sudden certainty that I was the crazy one. What I thought had happened could not have happened.

'Look, the reason I didn't want to come in is that there's nothing to discuss. There's no point in sitting down and talking about it. It's just over. I have nothing to say to you now that you know.'

'Why didn't you want me to come to your house? Why didn't you answer my calls?'

Silence, still glowering, as though I was being impolite, crossing some boundary of propriety.

'She's here?' I asked, voicing aloud what I had felt dirtying me for days. 'That's the only reason you came here, so I wouldn't turn up and see her.'

'It's not your business any more – any of that. It never was your business, in fact.'

I was weeping, and said, 'Just say goodbye to me then, if it's over. Can't you behave like a human being? Don't you owe me that?'

I didn't mean this, of course. I didn't want a goodbye, had no interest in a respectful parting. I only thought if I could make him concede, treat me like a person, touch me, the spell would be broken and he would love me again.

'Fine,' he said, his eyes still accusing, mocking. 'Goodbye.'

'Hug me goodbye,' I begged. I don't want to remember saying it.

He rolled his eyes and stepped towards me, patting my back twice, briskly, like a colleague might.

I grabbed him, clung to him, jammed my face to his chest, smelled him, gasping.

He brushed me off as easily as an insect and blew angry air and spit through his lips, swiftly scooping up his bag and opening the door, walking down the road at speed, not looking back to see me doubled over in the doorway.

He was gone. I dragged myself back inside and lay on the bed. He dawdled through the earth, fooling people into thinking he was alive. What had happened? I sat myself up and put my hand on the cool wall trying to stop the dizziness.

For the rest of the day I sat there and wept and muttered to myself the sequence of events that had led to this moment. I leafed through my diary to find the dates and then recited what had taken place, the day we met, the first time we kissed, the arguments, the reconciliations, the dinners. I said them out loud, again and again, start to finish.

5

My friend took his own life some years ago. A string of phone calls went around us all. I was working in a theatre at the time and ignored the call when it came through. A few hours later at a lunch with some colleagues in a pub, I got a text. It was from someone I barely knew, who didn't know my friend well either. I read it quickly, holding the phone in one hand as the food was being served and I was still half-talking to the others.

... sorry to be the one to ... died at home ...

I read it twice in quick succession, staring at the screen blankly. Then I put my phone away and ate my lunch. For an hour his death didn't exist in any meaningful sense. I can't remember a single conscious thought that passed through my head until we were all leaving and outside my knees gave out from under me and I stumbled against a wall, repeating: 'I think my friend is dead.'

A few days later, we gathered in his living room to drink and cry and talk about the funeral. We kept recounting events from the past few months, saying, '... and that was the last time I saw him,' to each other, insisting on describing the exact barstool we had seen him on, or gig we'd bought tickets to and why; as if to say to each other: It happened; I was there; did it happen?

January 2013
Dublin

1

When he left me, I went to the same faux-dive bar where we had argued about the poems written for Freja.

I wanted to be as fucked up as humanly possible, to obliterate the memory of his disgusted face on my doorstep. I kept seeing his bored and mocking expression. *You thought I loved you*, it said. *Ha!*

A succession of my girlfriends told me how much they had always hated him, how he was not good enough for me. I threw my head back and laughed, agreed. A friend of mine slid his hand on to my ass, pulled me towards him. I was nauseated by his wet whiskey lips slipping against mine. I pushed him away. It wasn't like that. It wasn't like that at all this time. I went home.

When I got in I collapsed into the armchair in which we had sometimes fucked. There was a night not long before Christmas when we had come home late after a house party, giddy and aroused. I put on a record and he had barely been able to wait as I did. He pushed me back on the armchair, threw my dress up over my face and put his mouth on the small childish bit of fat I was so afraid of, escaping over the band of my underwear.

'Get down,' he said.

And I slid out of the chair on to the floor in front of him.

I bit my lip, my underwear around my ankles, feeling him stalking above me. He liked to walk around with me like that – liked to smoke a cigarette and open a beer.

He pulled up a chair and sat behind me, watching me wait for him.

Later, I was filled with ecstatic confusion at how good it felt that he smoked as I went down on him. My entire body filled with incensed heat, making me work harder, be more fuckable, open my eyes wider, mouth wider.

There was something intoxicating about being insulted that way, the total lack of respect, the lack of acknowledgement that I was there with him. It was the feeling that I could have been anyone, or no one, that I was something to be emptied into or out, the feeling of existing only to receive what he had to give. When he came his hands flew backwards to grab the chair, his head flung back, eyes at the ceiling. Mine never left him.

I liked when it had been a day or two since he had last showered, this small act of sharing. When he had been cycling he would be covered in a thin film of soot from the traffic and the dirt and oil from his bicycle would rub off on me. I inhaled the warm, damp smell of his hair and put my face against his soft flannel shirt, to where I could smell the stale, sour, but somehow not-bad after-work smell of him.

Once he had finished complaining about whatever had irritated him that day or on his journey home, he would turn to me as though seeing me for the first time. He would still be wearing the ratty fingerless gloves and would put his hands on either side of my face, covering my ears, so I couldn't hear anything, and nor did I want to.

Once, he had asked me what sex smelled like, as I spent many minutes nudging different parts of him with my nose.

'It smells like a greenhouse,' I said, thinking of how it felt when we had finished and were lying beneath the blanket and the smell travelled up and was close and dense in that way, and gave the same feeling of infinite capacity.

2

Every moment of my day was saturated by his absence, each second made damp and collapsing and airless beneath it. I sat staring into space for hours at a time, unable to move beneath the weight. I enjoyed my pain because it made me less than ever. I was nothing but living nerves, a petri dish of matter. I had no characteristics outside of it.

Ciaran had hated that I was indecisive. He had hated when he would ask where I wanted to go to dinner and I would shrug and say I didn't mind and he should just choose. He hated when I wanted him to tell me what outfit looked best. He wanted me to grow up, to know what things I wanted and be able to say them out loud. He wanted me to not be the negative space which would fit in around his positive presence, and because I knew this, knew he might be able to truly love me if only I could be a real person, I failed even harder. I panicked and beamed great big bland incurious smiles beneath the frightening totality of his demanding gaze. I smiled and smiled until I cried, but still could not produce a single decision or statement to please him, to be convincingly myself.

And now he had left me and I was even less than that again – so much less. Now there was no thought that did not have to do with him and I did not want anything that wasn't him. I squeezed my eyes shut and thought of the things I would give for him to return. I could not identify a single thing in my life I would not sacrifice in an instant for him, any place I would not go. I could renounce every last person I knew, leave them to their lives which seemed only grey negatives of the real life I would be able to live with Ciaran. I would move with him anywhere on earth and need nothing.

I spent my time searching for everything I could find of him online. I made a folder where I deposited the most important items. All photographs of him made me cry, to come across one I hadn't seen before was so sad and beautiful that it made life seem almost good again. That there were angles of him I'd never seen, ways he was in the world I hadn't been around long enough to witness. It was so lovely and painful that I found it impossible to believe I wouldn't see them myself some day.

('When did you know that you and Freja would break up?' I had asked him once in our few discussions about her.

'I never did really,' he had told me. 'I still don't think of her that way. We had to leave each other, but you never know what's going to happen later. Life is long.'

Life is long. I refracted his words and bent them back to mean something good for me. You never knew.)

The best things I found were pictures of us together which I had never known existed. I was searching his friends' pages for news of him and came across a photoset from a launch in Project Arts Centre in Temple Bar. In one photo I'm wearing a thin grey T-shirt with a scoop neck and am pretty and flushed as I look up at him and laugh at something he says, his beautiful face cracked wide with glee. His hand is on my shoulder and I thrilled to see it there in public record, normally so strange about being physical in front of others.

There's something about a beautiful boy's face – not handsome, or attractive, or cute, but beautiful. Why are they so moving, when I see so many beautiful girls every day? It isn't fair, I know. A boy who is beautiful seems to have pushed through the mud and cement of his gender. His beautiful face seems carved out of the rawest materials.

There was something about such a face, in any case, which made me believe intuitively that the boy was good. If not on the surface, then in some other place you may have to dig down to find. I, who would have laughed at such a sentiment about a beautiful girl, who knew how fleeting and unreliable and meaningless our beauty was – I, still, was taken in by the beautiful faces of boys.

I looked for him online every day and murmured with feeling when I saw him in some particularly revealing pose; gnawing on his fingernails in the corner of a reading, looking flushed and uncomfortable at an opening speech during Dublin City Culture Night. I went back years and harvested what I could. I was friends with enough friends of his to have a good sense of where he would be most weeks, which openings he would go to and screenings he might attend. I didn't go to them, aware I would probably see her there.

Once I walked into a pub to meet a friend after work and thought I saw the top of his downy head peeking out of a snug in the corner. I swung around and messaged my friend to go somewhere else and ran down an alley that smelled of piss and had to press my temples with my knuckles until the pain blacked everything else out and my heart drifted back to normal speed.

3

The loss of someone you love can make you go mad in the best of circumstances. I did not just love Ciaran but loved him darkly, wrongly. Losing someone you love in those ways can turn you not only mad but wicked too.

When he left me, I dreamed of the two of them sometimes, woke up sweating.

I thought of going to his house and hammering on the window until they let me in. I dreamed that March of killing her and woke oddly calm, thinking repetitively: *Well, stranger things have happened; well, stranger things have happened.*

I had slipped into his room as they slept and stood looking at them from the doorway. Moonlight was on their faces and made them look beautiful and already dead. I wrapped her beautiful dark hair around my fist and cracked her skull against the wall – one, two – and because it was a dream I was strong enough to move her entire body in a violent wave with one hand.

Her mouth was opening and dribbling and bubbling and there was a black stain on the headboard behind, and her long thin arm was twitching and grasping uselessly until it wasn't.

Beside her, Ciaran watched calmly, his eyes raising to meet mine once she had stopped breathing, and then turned back towards the wall in the same position he always slept, dragging the blanket tight around him.

4

At night sometimes I called Lisa, the only person I could say the truth to, the truth that was so basic and so large.

'I need him. I need him,' I sobbed to her. 'I can't do it. I'm not able to do it.' Meaning to live, to go on living without him.

And I loved her for not bothering to contradict me or to tell me that I didn't need anybody, that I would get over it. She knew intuitively, knew always, that she herself did not need anybody to live, but this difference between the two of us didn't make my experience any less real than her own. She had seen how actual the need was with her own eyes.

When once I gasped, 'I'm alone, I'm so alone, I'm scared,' she didn't pretend that I wasn't.

'I know you are,' she agreed. 'You are.'

5

I looked for other people who had felt like me, hoping for comfort or clues. My search terms were things like 'Obsessive love', 'Famous cases of unrequited love', 'Incidents of obsession'. I read about a story I had heard first on a podcast years before, about a man named Carl Tanzler, a medical professional – though not a doctor – in Florida who had fallen in love with his patient, a Cuban–American woman named Maria Elena Milagro de Hoyos in the 1920s. She had suffered from tuberculosis, which had also killed one of her sisters. Tanzler was instantly obsessed with her, offering her his dubious medical expertise and radiology equipment, going to her family home to administer additional treatments. He showered her with gifts and jewellery and declared her the love of his life, the realisation of a series of visions he had seen of a mysterious dark-haired angel.

She offered no reciprocation. Her family undoubtedly must have found him an oppressive and disturbing presence, but allowed his advances so long as they had some potential to help cure her. But it all came to nothing and she died in 1931. Tanzler paid for the funeral and constructed a mausoleum.

In 1933 he visited the site of her burial at night and used a cart to remove her decomposing corpse, putting it in his car and taking it home. There he used pins and wires and ham-fisted cage-like constructions to keep her disintegrating bones together, and wrapped them with gauze and muslins heavily coated in fragrance to try to drown out the persistent stink of her decay. He made a mask, blank and smooth, supposed to replicate her real features but naturally terrible in its inadequacy. Neighbours saw him through his windows dancing with the figure of a woman.

He was brought to trial but never sentenced, and Maria Elena's body – such as it was, still dolled up with his horrifying artifice and inadequate mummification – was put on show in a funeral home where thousands of curious members of the public would go to view the spectacle. No peace for her, no dignity, even when finally released from her captor.

The first time I heard the story I felt angry. To demand ownership of a woman who doesn't love you, even when she is dead. To take that dead body and make it yours through hideous force, hideous care, hideous attention. It seemed to sum up all the ways in which men could take you without your permission and turn you into something you had never been, which had nothing to do with you.

Now, as I read it again, through my bewildered grief, I wondered if I was any better than him. I wondered if I ever had been. Perhaps I had just never loved someone madly until now. Perhaps I had always been as violent as a man. Wouldn't I do anything to reverse my loss, the absence of him? Wouldn't I sacrifice not just myself but himself to get it? Wouldn't I make him everything he wasn't, make him soft and tender and domesticated and weak, so long as it meant I could convince him to be mine again?

I read a case study of a woman, Patient M, who suffered from erotomania, or De Clerambault syndrome, in upstate

New York in the 1970s. The woman was the child of first-generation Chinese immigrant parents, and a diligent student at a Christian college. She had a strict but normal upbringing, supportive parents, friends, a handful of supervised dates with boys who were her cultural peers. In her sophomore year of college, she began to take tutorials from a Caucasian man – Professor X – in his early forties. The man was a professor of theology, and married with two children, all involved in the local church and community of which Patient M was also a part.

Patient M began sending letters of a personal nature to Professor X, telling him about her difficulties with her schooling, her family and other relationships. At first he replied, trying to offer her comfort and spiritual guidance, but quickly her correspondence increased up to ten letters a day, and he began to be alarmed by their overly familiar tone and strange references to affection and a shared bond he had no part in.

Though her family, her college authorities and eventually the police would warn her to leave Professor X alone, Patient M continued and in fact increased her campaign, perceiving their attempts to be proof of her theory that the professor's wife was determined to keep them apart. She began to stalk him at his office and his home, until she was expelled permanently. Her letters continued to show that she believed Professor X loved her and was kept from her only by the constraints of their Christian culture.

One July morning, professional acquaintances and friends of the professor were shocked to receive wedding invitations to the marriage of him and Patient M. The more distant of them presumed that he had been divorced and was planning a shotgun wedding to his rebound lover, before he got hold of them and explained the strange situation. It was at this point that Patient M was taken into institutional custody, after which her fate is unknown. Several weeks after her detainment as a mental patient, her parents received a phone call from a local Chinese restaurant, wondering where the wedding party was, for she had booked a sit-down meal for thirty to celebrate the union.

6

When Ciaran left me, I felt a comfort in how unendurable the pain was. If it couldn't be endured, it would not be. It would end soon, one way or another.

I went on living, going to work mostly (two days had been lost to the magnificent hangover which followed the night it had happened). Somehow my body knew instinctively to preserve itself for its future work. I ate well and minimally, and when I was inclined to cut myself I was overcome by lethargic refusal and never followed through with it. I was usually too tired to go out and drink, and too ashamed to do it alone. I had the feeling that by some obscure set of living rules I could graft my way out of the pain.

I talked to Lisa most evenings when the pain and boredom were overwhelming – it was good for there to be someone who didn't know or dislike him but who could nonetheless hear my loss. She posted me a care package filled with benign films and TV shows, and most nights I would fall asleep in the chair watching them, smoking a few cigarettes and nursing green tea. That sort of watching is almost as good as being drunk if you do it enough, the jokes mild, the story always much the same, the ending always coming good.

Every so often I would let myself become upset, would sit in bed with my back to the wall and head cradled in my knees. When the pain reached its pitch I would bang my head behind me twice in quick succession, hard enough to manufacture the feeling that my brain was being physically dislodged and to scare and then calm me. But those evenings were rare, and mostly I was too shocked to feel anything too intensely, for which I was grateful.

I listened to sad songs in the shower and cried along. Sometimes I would stop and see myself as from the outside and even laugh at such trite performances of heartbreak. I took the train to the south coast of Dublin once or twice a week to swim and walk around the brambly masses on the outskirts of Shankill. When I tried one day to stand at the pier on Dun Laoghaire and look out to the sea and reflect on my misfortune, I lasted only a few minutes before becoming self-conscious and retreating.

The feelings were real, but they could find no natural expression. I felt in Dun Laoghaire comically cinematic, swaying there in the grey mist. Was I feeling something true from within myself, or was I living out a fantasy I had assembled?

7

When I was fifteen years old I stopped eating and I became popular. Popular for me, anyway. The shockingly thin girls in my group at school – the ones who had Uggs and hundred-euro make-up palettes – had suddenly accepted me. It felt incredible. I would never be rich, but I could be with them, which was almost as good. Once we had a 'school dance', an expression of our desperate need to be American, and it was at the peak of my looking as much like a character in *The O.C.* as I would ever look. I planned my outfit for weeks, something that showed off my skeletal frame but also made me look Quirky, meaning only that there was a tutu on my dress.

I arrived to the dance and it was terrible. The boys were as boring, as childish, as ever. They did not resemble the boys in films, all played by twenty-five-year-olds, I had wanted to impress. The picture I had made in my head of me showing up and everyone turning to applaud my newfound beauty had not been realised. I went home. I had made myself an image and it had not worked.

My great-grandmother died in a nursing home. My father went to visit her there several times a week for years during my childhood and adolescence and occasionally I went with him. The place was as repulsive and frightening as you can imagine for a child, smelling of disinfectant or worse, and

I always left feeling like I had gone there to be good, to do something good, but had failed to achieve that.

Once I went outside ahead of my father and looked at the garden, and there was a rose there in the spring time which was so powerfully pink, with drops of dew clinging to it, that tears came to my eyes and all I could feel for one brief moment was the pure potential of life, and then I remembered where I was and who I had just seen, and knew again that the image I so longed to perceive meant nothing, was nothing.

8

When he left me, I didn't contact him, partly because I knew there was no point and partly because I was convinced that she would see any message I sent. I could not bear to think of them laughing at me, or worse, shaking their heads in sympathy. I knew that being quiet was the right approach – though what I was approaching, I was not yet sure; the correction of things, a return to earth.

I would not allow him to be gone from me for ever. That was why I was unable to mourn authentically, how I could keep from abandoning myself.

In April one evening I sat in my flat, restless as I used to be in the old days, spoiling for a big, messy night out. I couldn't let myself go, was too afraid and fragile still. I didn't enjoy seeing my friends, around whom I was forced to pretend that I was not in love with Ciaran and that I was angry at him for what he'd done. As a concession I let myself get drunk alone, and was opening the second bottle of red wine when the Bob Dylan song 'Don't Think Twice' started, a song he played often. A sadness that felt pleasurable in its fullness came into me and settled on my chest. Without thinking too much or anticipating a response, I grabbed my phone and messaged him:

Listening to Bob Dylan, thinking of you. I miss you.

His reply came a few hours later, by which time I had drunk everything in the house and was lying on my bed blindly watching television, saying only:

I miss you too

I held the phone to my breast and cradled it there like an infant. I clung to the heat of suggestion, I throbbed. A blissful patience swam through me, the certainty that I could wait for ever.

9

I would not have to. Three days later, days I filled with exquisite silence and restraint, he called me. He asked me to meet him outside the Natural History Museum the next day at two p.m.

I made excuses to go home sick from work and walked over to Kildare Street. When I turned the corner he was standing there, nervously pulling at the unravelled thread of his cardigan sleeve, by the same animal hedges where we had begun our first date.

When he saw me his face opened up and was full of light and my heart sang brightly in my chest. I had been right to wait, to be careful, to stay inside.

The spell had been broken and whatever he had been on my doorstep he was no longer.

I stood in front of him, my eyes soft with love, a smile of infinite tolerance and adoration. There was so much inside me that I wanted to give to him.

In that moment I was as happy as I have ever been, sure that the abundance and purity of love I felt was obvious in every way, through my waiting and my tininess, my forgiveness and willingness to be pathetic.

I was the woman. I had suffered. I was there.

'I thought we could sort of start again,' he said, and then kissed me.

I had won. And how did I win? Oh, in its way, it was easy – it was nothing; I was nothing.

Two weeks later, we moved in together.

April 2013

1

I filled our new apartment up with a slow, lazy satisfaction. We unpacked our belongings and arranged them together just so. Our books lived alongside each other, but did not mix, a mutual invasion too far even for me. He had three ornaments he set on the window sill alongside mine, a small stone figure of a mouse, a thimble and a pocket watch, all beautiful and delicate and precise.

I drew my finger over them and asked, 'Where did these come from?' without thinking.

A long time passed while he went on unpacking a suitcase, before eventually responding, 'A friend gave them to me.'

I knew what this meant and spun briskly away from the objects as though burned by them.

I never knew if he referred to Freja as 'a friend' in this way because he thought I was too dense to understand who he meant, or whether it came from a reluctance to say her name aloud, as if by doing so he would give her a way into our home.

Since we had reconciled, we had spoken barely at all of our separation, except in vague and soft ways about having missed one another. We behaved, both of us, as though an inevitable war had come between us and fate had intervened to bring us back together.

I had cleared up the most absolutely basic questions necessary on that first afternoon outside the museum: Is it over? Is she gone? Do you love me? Yes, yes, yes.

He opened his mouth to go on, and I kissed him again and would continue to do so when any malign words threatened to escape him.

We bought a blue flannel duvet cover, a casserole dish, a rug. At the flea market on a Sunday we acquired two amateur paintings of dogs which beamed back at us from where they hung in the bathroom, the charming incompetency suggesting some shared joke or history that we didn't, in fact, share. I shuddered with a thrill that could only be described as erotic while choosing a vacuum cleaner and bin. I felt proud and tearful every time I opened the wardrobe door, where his few pieces of clothing hung monastically next to my own bulk of old party dresses and garish sequinned sweatshirts.

2

It was the first time I had ever lived with a man, or shared a bedroom. It seems odd that there was no plan set out, no structure agreed to, about what we would do for one another and what we wouldn't. How did we expect to know how often the other would wish to have sex? How were we to decide who slept on the window side of the bed? And how did it come to be, for instance, that I was the person who cooked for us, without it ever being discussed? That something as vast and daily and necessary as eating became a responsibility that I willingly took on for him, and he willingly gave up to me?

It was the logical outcome. I was a good cook and he was not. I had to worry about my weight and he did not. I could taste, and he could not – not quite, not really. In any case, being dependent on another person's cooking always made me bristle. The idea of eating according to another person's whims, eating what doesn't necessarily accord with the other choices of my day, frightens me. He had no such reservations, food being a necessity which, so long as it was not overtly unpleasant, meant very little.

To me a food could be understood:

a) through whether I enjoyed it, and

b) through whether it made my body fatter.

Ciaran was concerned with neither. His judgements were derived on a purely moral basis. He was inclined towards singularity in all things. He would have preferred to eat a large bowl of steamed green leaves for dinner each day, if his big man's body hadn't demanded more.

For me, food was messier, more complex. It was stressful, yes, but could be joyful too, something to binge on, and then shy away from; something to wrestle with, and offer up, and bury.

When, as a pious starving teenager, I learned to cook, it was an almost holy process. Until then I could only deny or destroy what was given to me by others – the balled-up sandwiches at the bottom of schoolbags, missed breakfasts, puked-up spaghetti, chicken thighs mummified in toilet paper and hidden in my bedroom drawers until the stench escaped.

I learned to cook and everything changed. I was no longer merely a petulant schoolgirl who wouldn't open wide and take it like a good girl. I chose what I cooked and because I chose it and knew it intimately, I was able to eat it. I chopped peppers and carrots and green beans julienne and fried them in a little olive oil, I steamed sugar snap peas until their leathery pods split at the sides and ate them in front of the TV like popcorn.

When we moved in together, it had been a long time since I had pored over food in that way for myself. Something had broken in me when, as an adult, I had allowed myself to eat normally again and to gain weight. The betrayal of my thin self was too painful to confront fully, and so I refused to look food directly in the eye at all. To survive, I had to stop cherishing the individual slices of a polished pink apple divided up on a plate, had to stop finding them beautiful, or else I would never have stopped staring. I had to stop believing that the act of eating food

118

could do anything at all to my body, because if I didn't then I would never have been able to eat again.

I began to cook for Ciaran, and a measure of the sanctity returned, and because it was for someone else and not myself, I allowed it.

Living with him forced me to treat myself like a person in a way I was not able to alone.

At work, now doing entry-level admin in a dental hospital, I would spend lunches at my desk reading recipes, noting them down, eventually settling on one.

When I finished for the day, I would walk home and call into the good grocery place, the same place we bought apples to walk around with, and choose the ingredients. I trailed around the nicely lit aisles, which were overcrowded in a homely and pleasing way, brushing my hands against the overpriced olive oil, the dried seaweed, the rare kinds of honey.

I glided by the fish counter, mouthing the names of creatures I didn't know. The butcher sold me venison and when he handed over the package, bound nostalgically with brown string, the price made me swallow. I selected each part of the meal with tenderness and pride, to think of him eating it.

I had never shopped there before, would never have thought to. I had lived previously on what was discounted in Lidl combined with whatever tins I had in the cupboard, but my life was to be new now, and I shopped for it beneath the high ceilings amidst the other things I coveted.

It took a very long time for me to resent this part of our life. It was almost the last thing to go.

Along with sex, cooking was what I did to make it up to him – whatever 'it' happened to be that day.

He didn't demand or expect these reparations. I knew instinctively to use them. The ritual of the meal was offered up, something more intricate than usual on days I had offended him.

And afterwards, if I was able to have sex with him too, things were OK. When we had sex he forgave me, even when he didn't want to.

3

I remember the last meal I ever made for him, before everything changed for good, because it looked so pretty that I took a picture – crawfish and crab, arranged in neat pink scoops on top of lettuce leaves, lime juice and chilli, a spoonful of avocado, a sprinkling of black sesame seeds, and as I took the photograph, my phone lit up with a call from another man.

4

There was a time – which I realise now was such a brief time, almost nothing – when it felt to me we had triumphed over all the squalor that preceded our living together.

Before the real fighting began, and the worst he would say to me was, 'Why do you leave the sponge in the basin after you use it? Do you want it to get mouldy?' – mock-scolding me, wagging his finger, tossing the dripping thing at me across the room.

And I would squeal and shout 'YES!' and throw it back, and run shrieking down the hall, laughing in the bedroom as I heard him advance, stomping like a cartoon villain, and when he eventually threw open the door and rounded on me, he picked me up as easily as a pillow and threw me down on the bed and tickled me and we lay there squirming together until there was no breath left in us and we touched our noses together and fell asleep like that.

We napped together all the time, collapsing frequently among piles of sweaters in our freezing bed. The apartment was old, the ceilings high, and the heating whispered thinly out of the radiators to no effect. Droplets of water ran down the walls, and a dark stain crept threateningly across the bathroom ceiling.

Once we had eaten and Ciaran had put away any remaining work he had taken home, we would often go straight to bed. There we dressed in ridiculous sundry layers of thermals and pyjamas and old sweatpants, laughing at ourselves, and would hide beneath the covers watching crime procedurals and horror films.

I lived for this part of the day, both of us shivering still and kicking our limbs around to warm up faster, holding on to each other so tightly. That moment of dipping out of the freezing air and leaving the day behind, getting into our soft little palace, only us left in the whole world.

I kissed his fluttering eyelids where the veins showed and warmed the tip of his nose with my lips, and then he bent forward a little until even our foreheads met and felt sacred in their union.

I think, even now, if it was possible for me to have lived just like that, no other life coming in at the edges, no friends, no family, no work – if I had been successful in my attempt to boil my whole universe down just to us, burning bodies welded together in a cold bed – I could be happy there, still.

5

Then it was May and weak golden light filled our new home on weekend mornings. We woke up late, and yawned around together drinking coffee and chatting until lunchtime, when we would get newspapers and pastries and sit entangled on the couch, mindlessly petting one another as we read.

I saw my friends a little, for a glass of wine after work or occasionally for a film on Sundays, but none of them had been to our flat. I loved them in an abstract way, but was happy for our relationships to be remotely maintained with the odd message, a brief appearance at birthday parties. I was embarrassed in front of them, and they shy with me. I knew what they thought of Ciaran, could sympathise with their reasons. I didn't feel like suffering the further humiliation of trying to convince them he wasn't what they thought.

The truth was I didn't care what they thought of him, and Ciaran's own lack of caring strengthened my resolve.

'I saw your little friend Christina,' he'd say, after coming in from work, chuckling. 'I guess she doesn't like me, huh?'

And I would laugh along and roll my eyes, say something vague and conciliatory: 'Oh, you know what she's like,' and would enjoy the safe feeling of us both being against the same enemy.

It was the same feeling I had when he ranted about a rude colleague or someone cutting him off in traffic. At first I was inclined to soothe, to mitigate, because of how pointless it was to rail against them. Why get so incensed by these petty infringements when they were as inevitable as weather? But then I saw that siding with him was the safer thing to do. If I agreed with his outrage, and complained about the same things he did, we were by default teammates. He would begin to see me as not of the world that so angered him, but of his own world, the small one that we could build in our home together.

I was competent and efficient in my workplace, but only because I required a decent job to maintain the sort of life I wanted with Ciaran, not because I suffered from any ambition. I got through my days with a minimum of exertion, and was constantly shocked by how little actual work was accomplished in offices.

It was possible for me to spend only an hour or two a day doing my assigned work, and still finish the week with my assignments under control. After I had been there a while I realised the superhuman time-wasting skills I thought unique to me were in fact universal, and everyone was reading recipes or emailing friends or going for hour-long coffee breaks and calling them meetings.

When I unlocked our door each evening, my real life began, coming into technicolour focus. It rendered everything outside dull and irrelevant just like I knew it would, like I had counted on it doing.

Making a good meal at the end of a bad day can redeem the whole thing. No matter what else has taken place, if you have the time to do this one thing for yourself, it all falls away. It's not unlike the moment you sit down with a bottle of something strong if you're a drunk. You know there is a window approaching where the reality you inhabit will stop mattering, stop hurting.

My whole relationship with Ciaran was like that – a refuge, a singularity which obliterated other concerns. It was the best meal, the finest bottle of wine. As long as I could keep things going, as long as we could get along, the rest fell away.

6

I wonder now at my desperation to perform domestic acts for him. I wanted more than anything to present him with the products of my labour, for him to see how invested I was in maintaining our life – and how joyfully invested. I was even happy when I baked him a cake or cooked a meal, which he would then ignore or eat without thanks. I was happy when I washed a jacket of his which stank, unbeknownst to him, of cigarettes and weed. I was happy – I smiled, I sang! – when I scrubbed the toilet on my knees. The bleach smelled strong and delicious and burned the bloody creases I had bitten into my fingers and thumbs.

I wrote out meal plans and stuck them to the fridge with hearts and smiley faces and stars doodled around each neat entry, stretching weeks into the future – comforting to know already that we would eat a lamb kofte salad a month in advance, sweet to determine our faraway actions so precisely.

I wanted, I suppose, for him to need me, without knowing that it was me that he needed at all. I wanted him to live in a world where each need he might have had been preemptively filled. No button left unsewn, no white collar still ringed with browning sweat when he needed it clean. That's why I didn't need thanks. I didn't curse the absence of praise for my efforts. There was to be a whole functioning ecosystem surrounding him and he would have no cause to worry, or try, no cause to question anything at all.

It's easy to disappear beneath the incessant cycle of chores necessary to keep a pleasant and clean home. Women who once were individuals despair of being made into nothing more than wife, housekeeper, mother – a person whose identity is secondary to their ability to make things easier for everyone else. But I was not a mother. Doing everything for one other person, one man – in the heated flush of those first months we lived together, it felt sexy and intimate and even profound.

And after all, what individual had I been before? What identity was there to erase with my newfound house-pride? I had never found one resilient enough to live on in my memory once it had gone. There had never been one real enough to miss. I disappeared with perfect peace.

Was there even some feeling of mine that the whole dynamic was coated in a dusting of irony? Did that make it easier to love? The ludicrous idea of myself as a person who fetched slippers and roasted pork and made cold drinks for the big tall man in his overcoat smelling of outside evening, of real life that I was not a part of, it was so absurdly at odds with the way I had lived before.

If I thought that times had changed so much, that we were a modern couple after all, if I thought that my subservience could be ironised and eroticised out of reality – oh, I feel sorry for myself.

But I wanted it then – I remember the wanting, the greed for it, leaving work early so I would have time to prepare great midweek multi-course feasts, making his life into a production, a lively play of domesticity too loud to hear anything over. And when I was tired from it all and wanted to cry because I had got something wrong, a soufflé had collapsed, I had broken a bowl – or when he offered to help me – those were the few times I would become really angry with him. No, I would tell him, you just stay there and I'll take care of it. Meaning: you just stay there. I'll take care of you.

If he got something out of me, I was taking something from him, too. I was taking away his ability to live without me easily. I subbed his rent, I cooked his food, I cleaned his clothes, so that one day soon there would come a time when he could no longer remember how he had ever done without me, and could not imagine doing so ever again.

7

In June, when we had lived together for almost three months and the weather was warm, I noticed that I had begun to look at women as he would, as though I was inhabiting him. When we walked around Dublin together on weekends and the weak sun caused us to wear less, I began to see them through his eyes.

I had never been attracted to women in anything more than a passing way, but now I registered some of them in the same way I registered a handsome man. First it was only when I was with him – we would pass a pretty girl, I would notice her first, and my eyes would dart to his to see him clock her. Every time he did, I experienced it as a betrayal, but I also gloated inwardly that I had learned who would attract his attention in this way. What use I thought this knowledge might be I can't imagine now.

Soon it happened when I was alone, too. On my walk to work in the morning, down through Portobello and crossing over the canal where I passed other office girls and wealthy joggers, my eyes instinctively scanned for the ones he (now he-and-I) would like. There was no strict type in terms of ethnicity or colouring, but if I was to identify common threads I would say – delicate small features, maybe skewed towards the fashionably plain, large dreamy eyes, a suggestion of frailty and sensuality. Long hair, prominent collarbones.

I noted and stored them, regarding them with a twinge of prurient lust and the same helplessness I felt towards everyone he found attractive who was not me. There was nobody who was safe from this panic of mine. He referred once to his losing his virginity, fifteen years prior, to a beautiful girl named Jessica. For weeks after, I boiled. Jessica. Jessica. I wondered if I could find her through this forename alone, to stare at her, compare, rank.

When I gathered these women I saw on the street, filing them away internally, I was trying to protect myself as best I could. I was trying to build a registry of every threat in our vicinity, the better to prepare myself against them. But my mind had bled into his so that I wanted these women as he would have wanted them. So that the desire I regarded them with was lethargic and self-assured, as his would have been, and my mind wandered towards them in the invasive and probing manner I associate with the masculine thrusting of penetrative sex.

My gaze fell over them generally for a time, and then returned to its original target.

8

It was a Saturday in July when a far-right terrorist shot three people in Malmö. The gunman was dressed as a Catholic priest and had walked on to the grounds of Sankt Petri Church where office workers sat to eat their lunches on sunny days among the tourists and opened fire.

One of the three fatalities was a seven-year-old Japanese boy holidaying with his parents, the other two local women who worked in the vicinity.

Ciaran and I had come back from getting the papers and coffee when he saw the news online. The colour drained from his face and he stood up, muttering something inaudible at me, fumbling with his phone. He hurried out of the apartment into the hallway, where I heard him pace and then the low sound of his voice. I couldn't make out what he was saying. I stayed exactly still, staring into my coffee and down at my bare legs with the breath caught in my chest. I forced my eyes to stay open, unblinking and dry, until tears gathered in them. Freja lived in Malmö now, I knew.

It was insane for sexual jealousy to have entered my head even momentarily at such a time, let alone paralyse my entire body, but I was in love and so I was insane, and I can only feel glad I am at least no longer insane in that particular way, no matter what else I have lost alongside it.

He came back into the room, cheeks flushed slightly but otherwise normal, so that I knew no harm had come to her. He sat down without looking at me and opened the paper with a brisk shake like a father in a film at the breakfast table. I tore open the bag of pastries and put them on a plate, knowing already I would not be eating that day. I felt within me something I had not in many years, which was the desire to punish someone by not eating.

This was a regular inclination when I was young, an ineffectual but unignorable urge in the direction of someone who had wronged me. Most often it was towards boys who did not love me back or who did not love me in the right way, but it could also be towards parents, teachers, anyone, really, who failed to validate me in the way I required. It was never intended as a rational response; I knew, of course, that they would never know that I was not eating, and even if they did, they would not know it was they who had caused it.

That the pain was private made it better – I made them torture me, without their consent.

I took off the lids of our coffees and poured milk into them both unthinkingly – Ciaran took it black. 'Hey,' he murmured in protest, and, realising, I gripped the cardboard cup too tightly and spilled the scalding liquid across the table where it drizzled on to his lap and shoes. Horror filled my body and my throat swelled with it. He screamed – 'Oh what the fuck?' – and leapt backwards off his chair, brushing his trousers down.

'I'm sorry, I'm sorry,' I said over and over, and, 'Here,' as I grabbed a tea towel and tried to help. He kicked his leg to the side – not with violent intent, not to hurt me, but to get me away from him efficiently, as you might a dog.

'Just fuck off, can you?' he said and walked to the bathroom and locked the door.

I cleaned the spilt coffee off the floor on my knees and wrung out the rag in the sink. I boiled a kettle to fill a bucket so I could mop too. As it whistled I heard him let himself out of the apartment.

I walked over to the window and looked down at the street and saw him emerge, the sunlight glaring on his blond hair giving the impression briefly that it had caught fire, and he stalked towards the canal at a pace, no hesitation, as he always walked. I watched until I couldn't see him any more, and then I went into our bedroom, opened my computer and looked for Freja.

9

Freja has long fingers which arch through her dark shaggy bob in one picture. She looks right at the camera, or maybe the photographer, with a haunted intensity. She is leaning back against a chair splaying her legs like a man would, a pose which could only look beautiful on the elegant and thin. A man's white vest falls over her sharp bones and small perfect breasts.

Click.

In the next she is sitting in sand at sunset, drawing her hands through it to make shapes, squinting up at the photographer and shading her eyes. She wears a red paisley dress, which falls off one shoulder, and a pair of cowboy boots. She is smiling and her teeth are very white.

Click.

In another she dances in the corner of a bar, lit by the glow of a jukebox and a cigarette machine. Her head is thrown back, eyes closed, and she is wearing a black T-shirt and black jeans, hard classic clothes for a cowboy, which perfectly fit her hard girl's body. A cigarette dangles from her mouth – she looks like Patti Smith or a particularly pretty Manson girl.

Click, click, click.

10

I looked up Freja's accounts every day – in the morning on my way to the office, or sitting in the park with a coffee on my lunch break. I checked her Facebook and her Instagram and if I had time would trawl through her Google results and follow where they led me, hunt for clues.

I searched her friends, the ones who tagged her in pictures, to see if they had posted any others of her (they had), and to see what kinds of bars and restaurants they went to together.

The best was when Ciaran would go out on a Friday evening and I had the house to myself. He only ever went out alone on a Friday, when friends of his from galleries would meet after work to drink and eat pizza and gossip about shows and each other.

When we first lived together I would sometimes go with him but they were unbearably male evenings. I was often the only woman and got used to being ignored and spoken over. Occasionally, one of them would remember to be polite and turn to me with practised determination and say, 'And what do you think?' as though this was what conversation was. Once someone inclined towards me after I hadn't said anything for an hour as they chatted about a Hal Foster essay and asked if I'd read him.

'No, who's that?'

'A theorist,' he said kindly.

'I don't really like theory, I just do things instead,' I said, trying to make them laugh, which some of them did, slowly.

The part of me that enjoyed being an accessory to him felt gratified by the calm and stillness of sitting beside him in silence, no demands made of me except to be attractive and pleasant and friendly, but soon the boredom became too much and I stayed home instead.

Despite the vague dread of his being unfaithful to me, I came to look forward to these Friday nights. It was the only part of the week I was alone. Before, the idea of even an hour or two alone disturbed me, but now I was with Ciaran at nearly all times outside of work, and my Friday nights alone gave me space to look at Freja and to drink.

I got in at five or six, with a bottle of wine and a pack of cigarettes, opened my computer and put something mindless on to watch, something soapy with a lot of intrigue and sexual shenanigans, or reality TV starring a horde of blonde teens looking at their phones.

I put on my pyjamas, which were still Ciaran's old threadbare long johns and a T-shirt, and curled up in the corner of the couch. I poured a glass and lit my first cigarette and inhaled it and exhaled it and felt in that moment completely at peace. Then I would start looking at Freja on my phone.

A lot of the time it was going back over old ground. She didn't update very often and I had worked my way back through the four years of existing material. But I could never exhaust this bloody desire to examine her, to work my way inside her, to perceive her as he perceived her. I swiped through old albums which had pictures of Ciaran and her together.

My mind bent trying to look at these as an outsider would. I looked at them and then, as quickly as I could, clicked on to a picture of him and me together, trying to compare them to one another. Were we as well matched as they had been? Did we look as good? Did he appear to be in love with her, in a way he did not with me?

Because I knew that Freja looked at me too, I also looked at myself. I reviewed photos going back years and years. I tried to see myself as she saw me. I deleted the unflattering ones as I went, hot with the knowledge she had probably seen them already. As I looked at myself I pushed myself into her mind, the same way I pushed myself into Ciaran's when we passed girls on the street I thought he wanted to fuck.

By eight or nine p.m. I would be drunk, the TV show mumbling on in the background, chain-smoking, and knowing Ciaran would not be home for four hours or more I would go out to get another bottle of wine. Bleary eyed, I pulled on clothes and on my way down the street would toss the empty bottle away. He could find one the next day – he would expect this, and tolerated me being a drunk for one night a week. But two bottles would alarm and confuse him, would lead to a conversation, so I smashed it merrily into a skip, buzzed and lit with the comforting foreknowledge of the second one on its way.

2019, Athens

Before I had ever kissed a boy, I once walked for miles and miles with my most treasured childhood friend, Bea, reading her love poetry, from a book I had saved up a lot of pocket money to buy. She was cleanly beautiful like Freja. She was naturally tanned and naturally skeletal, like Freja. She had wide blue eyes set far apart, she had long limbs, she was so soft and good. Even then, when we were thirteen, she was much kinder than me. There were reasons for that – a person so beautiful has no reason to be cruel. How jealously I regarded her beauty, her cleanliness and smell of fresh clothes and the way that boys loved her and the way she was appropriately removed from them. I was always down in the dirt.

I envy women who are removed. I never really had that luxury.

11

I noticed after some months had passed that I now ignored the pointless spite he padded out stories with, instead of encouraging it as I had once, to prove I was on his side. The stories made me feel bored and hopeless.

Still, I responded to him with manic cheer. Sometimes I really was happy and untroubled and sometimes I pretended to be, and it grew harder and harder to tell the difference. It was as though he had vacuumed up all the available negativity in the apartment and I was afraid to let any seep out of me, lest it disrupt the balance.

After dinner we sat on the sticky leather couch and I listened to him noodle on his guitar, or watched him write in his notebooks out of the corner of my eye, anxiously, as I pretended to read, wondering if they were poems about her.

When he looked at his phone my heart went faster, I felt the blood moving through my terrible weak body, was completely unable to think of anything else. My eyes stayed fixed at a blank spot on the top of my page and then slowly leaked over into his space and I tried to peer sideways so hard my temples throbbed, to see if it was her he was speaking to.

I raised my hands to my mouth and began to gnaw on my fingers and thumbs, tearing thin strips of flesh systemically, grating them between my grinding teeth, swallowing.

Then we went to bed, where I wished we could be always, where he felt finally and truly mine, the friendliness of a body's smell and softness overpowering all the sour rest of him.

I greedily anticipated the luxury of whole undefined weekend afternoons of fucking and talking sprawling into evening, the shutting of the front door on Friday evening keeping trouble out and letting us become ourselves in private.

In my head, we woke late and lazily explored the limits of the bed and whispered and took care of each other until lunchtime. We read on the couch with our limbs intertwined and ordered in for dinner and drank wine and were back in bed by dusk.

There had been something like that once, something that made it feel possible.

There had been weekends when the containment of our apartment meant what it was supposed to mean – that we were good together when left alone.

There *had* been those times to prove to me that it wasn't my fault or his that he made me feel so degraded and sad, but the fault of the whole rest of the world.

If there wasn't a time like that (and I think just one would have done), how could I have believed in it so much, for so long, week after week, for months?

141

12

My father met Ciaran only once, when visiting Dublin for a funeral. He was always going to funerals, despite being significantly shy of sixty. He went to funerals for every person in his parents' peer group as well as his own, to those of old colleagues he hadn't spoken to in decades.

He went not out of the grim compulsion you sometimes see in people with not enough going on in their own lives, and not with any reluctant sense of duty. He went instead with a willing generosity of observance, a genuine desire to bear witness. He has always been good at seeing people, my father, which I think is why he has always been so well liked. He makes people feel that their lives are unique and worthy of interest, which, although true, is something rarely felt by ordinary people.

He had a few pints after the funeral – this one for a schoolmate he had been close with as a boy – and then met us in Neary's off Grafton Street. He was slightly drunk, which I could tell only from a fond mistiness in his eyes. He was warm and effusive with Ciaran, who was, I was relieved to notice, passably convivial. He was making an effort, and any of his natural coldness could be seen as mere deference to my father and me catching up.

We were mainly happy that day, Ciaran and I, and held hands and leaned close to one another when my father went to the bar to get us drinks. I noticed that his clear handsome face was in a state of constant and unusual gregariousness while we all chatted. Dad asked him about his work and he made self-deprecating jokes about his silly reviews while also subtly making it clear that he held some importance.

'My editor asked me recently to make my review of a show a little more glowing – old friends, you know? – but once you start down that path who knows where it ends, right, Thomas?' And my dad agreed, chuckling, as though he did know.

I was so happy that my father could see him this way. Towards the end of the evening I absent-mindedly chewed on a thumb hangnail and Ciaran took my wrist and withdrew it from my face without breaking his conversation with Dad. It was a thing I wouldn't have noticed or would have been even slightly pleased with, a cosy action, if we were not in company, but I met my father's eyes as he did it and dropped my hands to my lap, and then sat on them.

Afterwards, as he went to get a bus back to Waterford, my father hugged me and said he was delighted to have met Ciaran.

'And … are you always like that, so nice to each other?' he asked, and I was elated that this was the impression we had given off, that we were capable of such a thing, but then saw that there was something else in his expression, the gentle urgency of his face when I was a teenager and he wanted me to explain myself without wanting to force me to.

'Yes,' I replied. 'Always.' And he gave me a warm dry kiss, landing awkwardly between my eye and my mouth, and I turned away to go back inside to Ciaran.

October 2013

October 2013

1

We went to a film together in the old Screen cinema on Hawkins Street one Saturday night. I had looked forward all week to having a date with him, to dressing up and drinking afterwards. As we walked there Ciaran was relaxed and talkative and shrugged his overcoat óff one arm and draped it around me, containing us both inside, so that we were clinging tightly to one another as if in a three-legged race. We irritated others on the pavement and smirked about it.

The film was a rowdy drug thriller with Brad Pitt, and behind us a group of teenage boys shrieked sporadically and exploded with laughter when shushed. I felt the good mood evaporate from Ciaran and his body tense, sinewy and bristling. I searched out his hand to stroke reassuringly and he let it lie warm, dry, inert beneath my probing.

Each time the boys made a new noise my stomach lurched and I couldn't stop myself from sneaking looks at Ciaran until he whispered sharply, 'Stop looking at me,' and with-drew his arm from my lap. I stared ahead, panicked, wondering if I should suggest that we leave, but then the noise would lull and I'd think perhaps things were OK and could be salvaged, before they'd start up again hooting at an actress's breasts or a pile of cocaine.

'Should we move?' I whispered to him, which he ignored.

For an hour I sat still, dreadfully aware of each second passing, waiting for the next shout. When eventually the boys began to climb over their seats and rows and throw food at one another, Ciaran twisted around and said, 'Can you shut the fuck up please?' I squeezed my eyes shut as they jeered at him, repeating what he had said, exaggerating his accent and laughing uncontrollably. As ever, to be laughed at was the most galling experience for Ciaran, intolerable, and he stood up and left, exiting the opposite direction from me so that he did not have to involve me, take my hand to bring me with him or climb over me. I followed him, flinching from the triumphant crowing of the boys.

Outside he was lighting a cigarette.

'I'm so sorry,' I said.

'What are you sorry for?'

I didn't know.

'Let's just go get a drink?' I asked, pushing my arm beneath his coat and around his waist.

'Fuck that, it's Saturday night – everywhere's going to be full of idiots by now.'

I didn't say that it was the same Saturday night it had been before the film, a Saturday night in which he had been happy to go for a drink, had discussed with me which bar it might be earlier that afternoon.

'We could get some food and wine or whatever and bring it home, then? Watch something there or play some records?' I was getting desperate now and could hear it in my voice.

'What are you talking about? We had dinner before we left, why do you want to eat again?'

I didn't want to eat, or even very badly to drink, but only for there to be some thing that we were doing together that might bring us back to his good mood, an activity to give the night some shape and which might allow it to end with us having sex, resetting everything and making it bearable. We walked home in silence. I took his arm, which he allowed.

'Are you OK?' I asked after a few minutes.

'I'm fine,' he said and continued to look away from me.

'OK! Just checking,' I said.

Back at home he got changed into his soft clothes and took out a book and began rolling a joint.

'Will I make some tea?' I asked.

'Whatever you want,' he said, amiable enough now he was back inside.

'Do you want some, though?'

'I don't care.'

'I'll only make it if you're having some.'

'Why?' he asked.

'Are you OK?' I asked again.

'I'm fucking fine! Jesus!'

I turned away and made the tea.

'Did I do something?' I asked a few minutes later, after he had begun to read.

'What are you talking about?'

'You seem upset with me.'

'I'm not upset with you.' He kept his eyes on the book. 'I'm not anything with you.'

'Why aren't you talking to me?'

'Why do I have to be talking to you? I don't have to be talking to you to not be upset with you. Do I have to talk to you all fucking day and night? We live together, I'm here all the time, I can't talk for all of it just to keep you amused. Christ, it's like living with a toddler sometimes.'

I nodded, knowing that it was. I started to cry.

'I'm sorry, Ciaran. I'm really sorry.'

'What are you crying about? This is insane, you know that, right? You're making yourself cry right now, about absolutely nothing. You're crying about the absence of me being upset with you.'

'I'm sorry, I'm sorry, I know. Just – please, can you please, please—' And because I didn't know what the end of the sentence was, what I was pleading for, it just kept going, I kept asking, and asking, and asking.

2

My mother called to check when I'd be coming back for my birthday in November. Every year I went back home and had dinner with both my parents, a ritual they'd maintained since splitting up and during which they would harmlessly snipe at one another in a way I had grown to enjoy and be comforted by. It was nice to remember that they had existed together once and weren't always these now permanent versions of themselves, settled in middle age.

It was nice, too, to indulge the part of me which thought longingly of the three of us being united – this wasn't a scenario I wanted in any material sense, but one I thought of in the same abstracted terms as I thought of God and heaven, unreal but sacred. I didn't want my mother to leave Stíofán and beg my father to take her back and for them to be living in the same house; I just wanted a wishy-washy platonic ideal of us as a family. It was something I thought of when I thought about death, that if I had to die, I would want to sit with the two of them one more time together, to eat as our original, own family, that if I could do so one last time I would be able to feel peaceful and whole.

I told my mother I wasn't sure when I could come. I had gotten it into my head that Ciaran and I should go away on a trip, something we had never done before.

'What do you think about going away somewhere?' I asked in bed one night. I'd been looking at him fondly as he flipped through a magazine, shirtless, glasses on, hair damp, delicious.

'No money,' he said cheerfully. Sometimes it seemed to me that he took pleasure in the fact he earned so little, that his ability to live without comforts and luxuries so exceeded everyone else's.

'Well, we don't have to go abroad,' I said, winding a curl at the base of his neck around my finger and releasing it gently, again and again. The hollow gap in his sternum – I bent down and pressed my nose into it. 'We could just go for a weekend somewhere in Ireland.'

He stopped reading and smiled at my fidgeting around his body.

'You know, I actually do think I should see more of Ireland. It's dumb to move to a different country and stay in the same place all the time, right? I've only been here and to my father's.'

'Right!' I said, excited now and feeling the flush of intoxicating adulthood that a weekend away implied.

Maybe there would be a flask on the train, maybe I would wear something special – could it be that I was the sort of person who wore a hat?

In work the next day I looked at discount websites and hotel offers and finally booked a voucher for two nights at a bed and breakfast in Galway for the weekend of my birthday. I packed swimming things – I was proud of the fact that I could go in the ocean all year round – and a new black dress with a deep neckline and pearl buttons at the waist. On the train there my heart hurt at the sight of Ciaran's happiness.

'I love trains,' he kept murmuring, gripping the window excitedly as he watched the scenery, and sliding his other hand over to me, squeezing my knee. I stared at him and when he looked back he crossed his eyes and grinned wider, mocking the fact of his own merriment. We did a crossword together and drank coffee and ate chocolate bars and he said, 'Why does coffee taste so good with sweet things?'

In Galway it was freezing and clear skied and gorgeous. I said we should go to the beach while it was still bright out and as we walked to Salthill along the promenade I saw that he was happier still. I remembered that he really hadn't seen much of what makes Ireland itself. He spent all his time being irritated by the mundane city things of Dublin, things that were generically urban and had not much to do with specific location.

'We should go places more often,' he said.

At the end of the prom on the Blackrock diving board I took off my backpack and coat and he laughed.

'You're not seriously going in there, are you?'

I raised my eyebrows and kept undressing to the bikini I had under my clothes and he joked around trying to bundle me into his jacket. It really was too cold and if I had been alone I would have left it, but his disbelief was inspiring a hysterical bravado and there was no turning back. An elderly couple strolling were looking as well and I laughed with the attention and the shock of the wind on my bare body, and then I ran and jumped.

When I surfaced I gasped for air that didn't seem to come and waded until my heart slowed back down a little, then thrashed perfunctorily for a few minutes. I looked up and he was smiling down at me and shouted, 'Brava! Brava!'

When I climbed out he was waiting to surround me with a towel and my coat and he licked the salty water from my ears and said, 'You're beautiful.'

Afterwards we got a taxi to the hotel, which was further from town than I had thought it would be, but perfectly nice once we arrived. We showered and wore the fluffy robes for the novelty for a few minutes, before we started to kiss and shrugged them away to grab on to each other. He stopped me when I trailed my hand downwards and said, 'No. I want to save it for later. I want you to want it all night.'

And my head was light. I bit my lip and breathed in sharply.

He had packed nice clothes and I felt touched watching him dress, a beautiful soft pale blue shirt and a white tie, and he looked so handsome, so sharp and manly but heartbreakingly delicate that I wanted to photograph him, or paint him, make him model for me all night instead of going outside. He looked like an illustration of superiority, like propaganda for the idea of a man.

I had chosen to take him to a restaurant run by a friend of Lisa's, a woman whose whimsical charm was so eye-wateringly acute I could barely speak to her. She was the kind of person who ran dinner events full of the best looking people you'd ever seen in your life, in bogs and old vacant military barracks, using only what she had foraged in a 50-foot radius to cook with. I told him about her on the walk and he said, 'Oh wait, I've heard of her; she does collaborations with an artist we interviewed in the magazine last month.'

I felt clever and proud to have done something related to his interests without even meaning to. At dinner he admired the sparse room with its handful of tables. It was like restaurants in Copenhagen, he said, and happily if thoughtlessly ate everything on the tasting menu. If Ciaran couldn't taste food with as much enthusiasm as I could, I had reasoned when choosing the place, he could at least enjoy the aesthetics of her plates, artful piles of tweaked sprigs and things you would not expect could be pickled, but it turned out could, and minuscule sea life I had never heard of before.

On the street after, tipsy from some strong seaweed-flavoured cocktails, I asked, 'What now?'

'Let's go for a drink. I want to go to one of the real old-man pubs with the nooks in them,' he said.

I took him up to Tigh Chóilí and he stood behind me as we waited to be served, one arm around my waist and one hand brushing my thighs under my dress so that I was flushing giddily, and that's when I saw him. A man from Waterford I had dated a little bit in my late teens and then slept with on and off during the odd Christmas holiday or summer festival was serving behind the bar. Michael, a little older than me, a sweet person who played drums and didn't have a huge amount going on but liked to drink and was friends with my friends from home and was nice to me.

'Michael!' I said and jerked reflexively to remove Ciaran's hand from beneath my dress.

We caught up for no more than thirty seconds – he had moved to Galway, yeah, it was very busy in here, time goes faster that way anyway, though: can I get two pints of Guinness? – and I turned back around, smiling broadly, heart thudding. I was afraid to find what I knew I would find, which was that things had been ruined in the space of that minute, that I would spend the rest of the night trying to claw my way back to the good feeling, and that I would fail. We stood in silence, being jostled by the crowd, waiting for our drinks and then moved out to lean against a wall.

'Who was that?' he asked.

'He's a friend from Waterford.'

'Why did you move away from me when you saw him?'

'I didn't – I ...'

'You did, yes. You moved away from me as soon as you saw him. He's a boyfriend?'

'No, no, nothing like that.'

'Someone you fucked, then?'

I said nothing, grew hot.

'You're blushing,' he said, mocking. 'You fucked him?'

'It's nothing, he's nobody important.'

'What's nothing? It was nothing when you fucked him?'

I looked up at him, agreeing miserably in silence.

'Unbelievable.'

'It's not a big deal, Ciaran; you've slept with other people too, haven't you?'

'Yes and yet we don't bump into them in totally random places, there aren't so many that they pop up from behind bars in different cities.'

'Please.'

'Please what?'

We drank in strangled silence for a few minutes.

'I'm sorry. Please can we just forget it and have a nice night?'

'Fine,' he said, but wouldn't speak to me or look at me, and when we were done said he wanted to go back to the hotel. We couldn't find a taxi and the walk seemed to take for ever, cutting through pitch-black mucky fields.

'Why is this place so fucking far away? We couldn't have just stayed in town?' he asked, and I tried not to apologise again, knowing it would make things worse.

When we got there and went to our room he undressed and shut off the light as I was still doing so, and I got into bed gingerly, facing his turned back, and reached out to touch him. I worked the knots of his shoulders and stroked his neck and then moved closer to him, putting an arm around his waist and touching beneath his T-shirt.

'Stop it,' he said, not moving. 'Just go to sleep.'

'I can't go to sleep with you angry at me.'

'I'm not angry with you.'

'If you aren't angry with me why can't I touch you?'

'I don't want you to touch me. Not wanting you to is reason enough, isn't it?'

'Of course, just, let's talk about it and we'll figure it out.'

He made no response, his breathing even and deep.

156

'Just tell me what you're thinking and it will be OK,' I said, but there was nothing.

The insult of his ignoring me struck me suddenly and made me recoil, taking my hands from him and returning to my side of the bed. I started to cry, filled with self-recrimination and grief for our lost trip, silently at first and, as I went on, wetly, snivelling.

I could feel that he was awake and feared or hoped he would reprimand me for crying and making noise but he remained that way, turned away from me, long and still tense and blank.

3

Many nights I spent doubled up on the bathroom floor. I didn't lock myself in to protect myself from him. I did it when I had begged him to forgive me, answer me, acknowledge me, and he would not. Sometimes this lasted for hours, and to punish us both for that humiliation I locked in and began to cut myself.

'What are you doing in there?' I imagined him saying, knocking on the door. 'Please, don't hurt yourself.'

I wished he would do as an old long-ago boyfriend once had – had grabbed my scarred and crusting forearms together, which were then as rickety and pale as ossified twigs, and looked me urgently in the eye and said, 'I want you to promise me you will never do this again.'

4

Or even to do what a man working in a department store had once done, which was to turn away from me in disgust.

I was fifteen or so, shopping with friends, and the most manically able to endure pain as I ever would be. Nothing seemed to touch me, no matter how I tried.

When the man floated past, offering samples of a Marc Jacobs perfume (which I remember as also being embedded in the nightmarish beauty of that time in my life, the long-legged anorexic icons of my youth, who decorated my walls, the flowery vaguely sickly glamour of it infecting everything it touched, Mischa Barton, Nicole Richie, size zero and enormous It bags), the girlfriends I was shopping with accepted wordlessly, only half paying attention, still idly browsing with their free hand.

I did the same, thoughtlessly proffering my wrist while looking away at some feathered dress I coveted, and when the man went to spray the scent, he gently pushed up my sleeve and sprayed automatically, too late to stop by the time he registered the open wounds he was spraying into.

He gasped and looked at me with curious revulsion, and I yanked my arm back and pulled the sleeve over the cuts, which were now burning alarmingly. I kept shopping, but was sullied by the judgement.

5

But nothing came from Ciaran. Nothing came, and it had become impossible to hurt myself with the convincing rage I once had. I had grown reflexively weak and self-protective, not able, as I was back then, to harm myself without thought, without fear of the pain that would follow whenever I showered or dressed in the days to come.

Inside me things were boiling and rupturing and sprouting, and twenty feet away he sat looking out the window, calmly smoking, with a book resting on his lap, an indefinite horizon of stillness, silence. A great fear swelled in my chest as I crouched there holding my body, my body, which felt to me so much to blame for everything that happened to me. In these moments I knew that if I could be smaller, smaller, less and less, if I could be tidied, then he would love me fully and properly; and that anybody – oh, everybody – would.

That knowledge, which felt as clear and undeniable as laws of science, as nature, as the fact I had a body at all, drove me mad. It fizzed in my brain, frustrating me with its nearness and impossibility – because I knew from experience that although I could approach it practically, with calories and carbs and sit-ups, there would never be a bone sharp enough, a size small enough to let me reach the place I wished to get to.

6

It wasn't that, on balance, there were more good times with Ciaran than bad, and that's why I stuck around.

There is no better feeling to me than to wake up in the middle of the night and thrust my hand out and say, half in a dream still, 'I love you so much,' and for a person to turn towards me from muscle memory and say through their own sleep, 'I love you too.'

There's never been a drug or a friend or a food that's even come close.

7

People at work thought me odd and treated me with friendly suspicion, but I was unfailingly pleasant and even almost well liked, smiling and willing to nod and chat about someone's kids, or take on extra tasks for people who wanted to leave early.

When I refused the endless boxes of chocolates and biscuits that were passed around, they lauded my amazing self-control, and chided themselves for their greed. I grinned and rolled my eyes in a self-deprecating way and turned back to my computer screen (where I copied and pasted long articles into documents and emails so that I could spend all day reading, while looking at a glance as though I was busy).

I didn't know what to say – how to explain that I would rather shit in front of them than eat chocolate in front of them. How could I explain such a thing, the shame it would bring me to participate in the office food chat?

Or that I would prefer that none of them knew much more about me than my name and the area I lived in and that I more or less adequately performed my job?

I didn't want them, their sticky over-familiar comments, on me. I dreaded for them to see what I ate, to know what went inside me, because the more they knew the more I would be forced to sincerely inhabit the role I was playing, the harder it would become to tell the difference between the me in there and the me at home.

8

My friend Christina would sometimes call. I saw her and a handful of the others maybe once, twice a month, always straight after work and for no more than two hours. When I left I didn't say why I had to go, or where, and they didn't ask.

Once she called on a Friday night when we had nothing planned, when I had just got in and was readying my bottle of wine and pack of cigarettes and laptop and phone to curl up and drink and look at Freja and watch shitty television.

'Come on, it's just a small thing but everyone will be there and you should come. When was the last time you came out properly?'

We both knew that it had been a year or more now since I had spent a full evening with anyone but Ciaran.

'Come over now,' she said, 'and we can get ready and have drinks here and go together. Anyway, you have to come, Lisa's home from Berlin.'

It gave me a funny dreamy pain in my chest to hear this and to think of Lisa.

It seemed a different lifetime in which we had lived together. I thought of her goofy face and the earthy smell of her leather jacket and the endearing swagger of her walk, so incongruous with her small self. I thought of the way we had lived together. We were autonomous, could happily go whole days without speaking to each other, me reading on the couch and her drawing at the table, passing cigarettes back and forth. And yet there was such pleasing self-containment, too. The combined force of ourselves made the silence rich, made the rooms we shared into a home. We had done together what I had never managed to do with Ciaran.

But still. I couldn't go out. I couldn't be absent when Ciaran arrived in or, worse still, couldn't be here and pissed when he did.

'N – no,' I replied to Christina shakily, and heard her impatient sigh blown out the other end.

'But tell me what you'll do. I want to know what you're going to do.'

And I closed my eyes and breathed slowly and let her tell me how exactly the night would happen, although I knew it already.

They would drink wine and prosecco in Christina's flat, put on make-up. They would go to the pub at ten and smoke Marlboro Menthols and drink rum and coke or G and Ts or more white wine. They would go around the corner to the Workman's Club and stay there till closing as long as it wasn't full of arseholes and as long as nobody's ex was there with someone new. They would spend lots of money on poorly mixed cocktails.

They would go to DiFontaine's for a pizza slice on the way home. The staff would turn the music up and let people treat it as a little post-club party so long as nobody got carried away.

And then, if everyone was up for it and not too tired, they would head back to someone's house and take pills or lines of coke and drink more wine and listen to music and smoke a million more cigs and fall all into each other on the couch, laughing and dancing and maybe some people kissing, and they'd stay up till six or seven at least and if it was a particularly good buzz someone would pop down to the shop then and get more booze and they'd go all day, but otherwise they'd all get a few hours' kip and then drag themselves up at midday to go for food, all bedraggled and smeary-eyed, and laugh about what idiots they'd all been the night before.

She finished and then a soft click as she hung up.

9

One Monday night I peeled potatoes over the sink, ready to mandolin them into thin slices and bake on top of a pie I had read a recipe for in the newspaper on Saturday. It had been an unusually calm weekend for us. When, at a certain point, Ciaran had stopped speaking or responding to me for no reason I could work out, I felt less agitated than I often did, and went to our bedroom to read. The next morning he was pleasant and affectionate and I thought with disinterest how little I could comprehend the move-ment of his moods.

I was tired from working, that Monday evening – it was a day with more meetings and compulsory speaking than most – and my back ached from the way I was always hunched tightly over my screen, not realising I was doing it until it was time to leave and I felt that all my muscles had cemented together and had to be prised apart.

A dull ache spread in the base of my spine as I stood at the sink, and I was suddenly livid. I didn't want to be standing there, on my own, preparing food for another person. I craved with visceral, addict thirst the experience of buying a frozen pizza and a bottle of wine and not thinking remotely of anyone else.

I wanted with a frightening violence the blankness of that evening, which I had wasted so many of in the past, not appreciating their luxury.

It's a peculiar anger, resenting doing something that nobody asked you to do. And it's a peculiarly impotent sort of anger that domestic labour brings about. It was building up in me, a feeling like the blood of my body slowly becoming dirty as it coursed through.

With every strip shorn off the potato I cursed him and the apartment, even though as I did so I knew it was I who had begged – quite literally at times, had begged on my knees – for the privilege of living in this place with him, in this exact manner. It was I who had been so anxious for domesticity, for the reassuring sameness of our shared routine, for the comfort of knowing that it was me he slept with every night.

I had begged to be standing there over that sink, had begged for that very potato, slimy in my grasping hand.

I heard him come in, speaking on the phone. Heard him shrug off his backpack and hang his coat and walk into the bedroom. I halted my peeling for a moment and strained to hear his voice. The words were unclear but I could make out from a particular tone that he was speaking to Freja.

What was this tone? It was not quite flirtatious. If it was, I would have been more emboldened to object to their semi-regular conversations.

It was, if anything, a cautious tone, careful and reticent. But, unmistakably, there was a softness underneath it which I only ever otherwise heard directed to me, a surrendering shyness absent from his usual ready-to-go spiels that could be fired out at gallerists or artists or journalists or friends at will.

And it hurt me and fascinated me because it was so beautiful to hear.

It was so much clearer to hear when it wasn't for me, because when I heard it I couldn't help but dissect and worry over it, prodding it to mean more than it did, or investigating it for sarcasm. Separate from me I could hear its reality and that there were other parts in Ciaran than the cold and forbidding ones. This reality saddened me because it meant I wasn't myself able to bring them out; or worse, it meant they were as far out with me as they ever could be.

He was careful not to speak of her too much or to behave as though she held much importance. She was forcefully relegated to the same status as several other friends in Denmark he spoke to every few months. The only thing that could goad him out of this neutrality was news of her promiscuity. She would drop into conversation that she had slept with some mutual acquaintance of theirs, or a friend of Ciaran's would laughingly inform him of her alluringly seedy exploits – the club she was thrown out of for being found on her knees in the men's bathroom, the time she fucked a guy in a park before wiping herself off and going to meet another date.

He fumed about these to me, wondered aloud why she couldn't get herself together, why she didn't respect herself. I never knew what to say, torn between wanting to encourage his disgust and the awful feeling of his still-present connection to her. And, too, it amazed me to conceive of her out there in the world living luridly but still the object of his love and fascination. I was here, in the home, safe and useful as a sink.

I stood suspended as they talked and when he began to softly laugh at something she said I pressed the sharp blade into my thumb for as long as I could and then quickly tore it downwards. I bled into the wet colander of peeled potatoes, until Ciaran emerged from our bedroom and I showed him that I had ruined dinner.

'That's OK,' he said, sitting down with a book. 'Let's just order something.' And I turned back to my mess, furious, boiling, wanting so badly for him to be angry with me.

10

Ciaran didn't like me to be drunk, a fact I had always known and accepted in the same way I accepted that he didn't like eggs, or modern fiction – just one of those things. It didn't much matter until later, in any case. For the beginning of our relationship and the beginning of our living together, my primary desire was to please and be loved by him. It wasn't my only desire but it shadowed all the others, so that when I wanted to drink and Ciaran didn't it was filed away neatly, not causing me any worry.

We were grocery shopping in the Lidl near our place one evening that November. He didn't like to come with me and he annoyed me when he did – someone who doesn't like food will not respond convincingly when asked to evaluate different kinds of lettuce – but I had taken to insisting that he did.

'I'll be bored otherwise,' I would say, but what I meant was, 'I want you to be bored too.'

I didn't see why he should get away with so much.

(I must remember, keep remembering, that he never wanted it, never wanted it, never wanted it – I begged him.)

I had my meal plan for the week noted down and was checking off ingredients when we passed the wine aisle and I felt an itch.

'I want to have some wine with dinner,' I said to him. 'Do you want a beer or anything?'

I kept my eyes away from his, scanning the shelves, so that he wouldn't be able to silence me just by looking.

I was trying something out.

I wanted him to have to explain it, out loud.

'No,' he said, with a little surprised disquiet – it wasn't a weekend, when I might be expected to say such a thing. 'Don't get wine, it's a Wednesday.'

'Why not?' I asked, still facing away, brushing the labels of the Rioja with a testing finger.

'Because … it's not good for you,' he said, and he was trying something out himself.

This was a kind of victory for me.

He had never had to say aloud why he didn't like it before.

Now he had been forced to come out with something concrete, a thing that could be reasoned and argued with.

I turned back to face him, innocently.

'But you don't mind that I smoke?'

Ciaran smoked. Ciaran was what my mother would call a 'real smoker', as in, a couldn't-go-a-day-without smoker, a smoker who got antsy on aeroplanes.

I smoked endlessly when drunk, it was true, but wasn't bothered with cigarettes in between. They were the same as drinking to me, a kind of full stop to thinking and daily life, an end-of-the-day excess.

'Why doesn't it matter that I smoke, if it matters that I drink?' I went on blankly, enjoying his discomfort.

'It's … smoking is bad for you, yes, but drinking interferes with things, stops you functioning as well.'

'I won't be hungover from half a bottle of wine, or even a bottle of wine,' I said. 'I'll be fine. You know my job is easy.'

'Do what you want,' he finished irritably and stalked towards the tills. I had won something from him, I knew, even though I would pay for it in silence.

At home I poured myself a glass while I cooked and drank it slowly, smugly, as he ignored me.

When we had finished dinner, I went on drinking as I read my book until it was time to sleep and I rinsed the empty bottle carefully and put it in the recycling bin as he watched me from the couch.

I thought this event would weaken his position, the hypocrisy of it coming from someone who smoked all day long, but in the end it bolstered him. He decided to double down, that health concerns made his distaste unimpeachably legitimate.

He emailed me studies about young professional women developing cirrhosis, and charts with the number of calories in each drink. When I lingered over some fine line around my eyes in the mirror he would lean over my shoulder and explain that drinking would age me faster, finishing with a cheerful kiss to the top of my head.

Before long it had spread to other parts of our life, too. He chided me on the mornings I got a bus rather than walk to work. If I complained that an item of clothing didn't fit me any more, or wept with sadness at the state of my body when in the middle of a depression, he would patiently explain that I would lose weight if I went vegan – Freja was a vegan, after all.

Once he went to see his dentist to get some fillings done and came home extolling the virtues of flossing.

'I don't want to,' I would say as he tried to force it on me in the mornings, wriggling out of his grip and trying to get out the door to work before he got his shoes on and caught up with me.

'I don't CARE if you do it or not,' he screamed at me once, 'I just want you to understand this, understand what I'm telling you: one day your teeth are going to fall out of your fucking head, and it will be your fault, not mine.'

One cold Sunday morning, getting ready to go for a walk into town, eat lunch, and go to the cinema, we stood next to each other, him shaving, me brushing my teeth. We were in good moods, him winking at me in the bathroom mirror when we caught eyes.

I spat into the sink and went to rinse the foam away but he seized my wrist and held it still on the tap.

'Do you see that?' he asked.

'Wh-what?' I cried, alarmed.

He peered down into the spit and then took a finger and dispersed it, combed through it. A thin, bright red strand ran through.

'Blood,' he said. 'That's blood. That's disease. That's what happens when you don't floss. Do you see now?' And he cupped the back of my neck, not unkindly, and slowly forced my head down close to the spit, so I could see it clearly; it was an inch from my nose; I felt my throat rise.

See?

11

I drank more in front of him from then on, a beer or two before dinner most nights, wine towards the weekend.

I was rarely drunk, and that was a part of it. If I crossed over into sloppiness as he sat there sober, I would lose the game entirely. His unspoken point would be proven. But if I could drink and maintain composure, he would have no basis for his evident disgust.

There were things about me he could legitimately criticise. I never exercised, was as sullenly unfit as I had been in PE as a child. When he chided me for this (he who cycled everywhere and could run for miles), all I could do was lower my eyes and say, 'I know, I know.'

But the drinking was different. If I forced him to become angry about it, it would make him look ridiculous. I was acting comically poised, after all. I was sitting reading the Sunday supplements, having cooked him a nutritious and inventive meal, holding a civilised glass of fairly good wine, the only untoward or slatternly thing about me the blush which arrived from the alcohol and the faintly sexual thrill of inciting his irritation.

Then I came home to him pouring bottles of wine down the sink one evening, and was quietly delighted.

When I asked what he thought he was doing, he answered that he wanted to make new rules for the house.

He wanted us to cut down on smoking, he said, for our health and because it made the apartment smell bad. And since I only ever smoked when I drank, we would simply make it a rule that smoking – and therefore drinking – was permitted only on one night.

Just one – I could choose which.

'What about you?' I asked.

'Yes, me too,' he replied, and I almost laughed aloud that he was willing to do this to himself.

'Fine,' I said. 'Good idea, baby.' And I kissed his soft unshaven cheek, rubbing my nose along it.

Usually I got home an hour or two before Ciaran did and it occurred to me that it was possible for me to drink before he arrived and to continue once he had.

If it was a night when drinking was allowed, I could, for instance, be home with two bottles of wine by five thirty, drink the first, dispose of it, and be sitting waiting for him with the first glass poured and a cigarette lit when he arrived home.

The almost-full bottle would be waiting there alongside me to prove everything was in order. I could easily suppress my drunkenness in front of a comparative amateur like Ciaran.

And so that is what I did. Sometimes if I was running late it was a struggle. I remember draining the end of a bottle of rosé prosecco in one burpy rush, my eye on the clock, and running down to the dumpster with only minutes to go.

But at night, when we had finished watching films or television, and he had had his beers and I had finished my second bottle, when we were going to sleep – it was all worth it then. I closed my eyes and felt the blissful wooze of being secretly, silently pissed, and of getting away with it, of being one person, and also another.

And then it was Saturday afternoons. I began to invent a social life for myself.

'Christina wants to have coffee with me today,' I'd say, or, 'Lisa is back from Berlin so we're going to see a film and have dinner,' and he'd barely look up from what he was writing or drawing or the application he was filling in.

It occurred to me uncomfortably that he hadn't stopped me seeing my friends, as I sometimes posited in the privacy of my own head. He didn't care about them. I had stopped myself.

I would get ready, get really quite dressed up, in flippy dresses and soft cardigans and little boots, would pull on my hat, put on red lipstick. I did my make-up perfectly, as I rarely bothered to do any more, and walked to a little bistro named Chez Max at the foot of Dublin Castle.

Lisa and I had come here a lot when she lived in Dublin to drink their house red and share onion soup and fries, smoke too many cigarettes.

On my walk there I would buy two newspapers, fat with supplements, and arrange them in front of me on the table, would sit down beneath the heat lamp, take off my coat and lay my cigarettes next to the papers. I nodded to the waiters, who knew my order. I sat there all afternoon slowly drinking wine and smoking and reading.

They treated me like a celebrity because I came so often, on my own, and had visibly made an effort to look pretty. I couldn't tell if they admired or pitied this but I didn't mind. It became the part of my week I most looked forward to.

Why didn't I actually meet the friends I said I was going to? I could have, they were still around, were still willing to see me when I asked.

It wasn't that I didn't want to see them. It was that I wanted it to be not true, where I was. I wanted there to be a thing he could not know.

12

Sex with him began, slowly, to fail to excite me.

His body was still as remarkable, as porelessly beautiful, as it had ever been. I could still spend hours exploring it, marvelling at its effortless grace, its movie-star glow. And yes, it was true, I could still forget everything momentarily when he lay there dormant or near sleep and let me burrow down and run my face against the insanely soft fuzz of his strong, long thighs. He felt the same, tasted right, smelled as good.

But there was something unreal to him, doll-like almost. I struggled to feel his touch. Things he used to do which would render me a quivering strand of pure feeling barely registered now. It was a strange thing to have his long beautiful fingers brush circles on my nipples and remember quite clearly how it once would have made me senseless with need, but feel nothing much at all.

I was able to perform my passion, having learned the movements so long ago, but it shocked me that he couldn't tell the difference when I shuddered and gasped my way through a faked orgasm. I might have been doing it all this time, I thought, for all he knew, and felt both proud and frightened of my aloneness, of the impossibility of being known.

I could only get wet when I went down on him, placing his hands behind my head, encouraging him to use me like that. I looked up at him and then could gather some of what I'd once felt; the power of that male sneer, that old faithful angle.

He was a little rough at times, but I could sense he did it out of kindness, knowing it was something I liked.

When I had once told him that I liked men to be rough with me, I had stopped short of describing exactly what it was I liked, or why, and what about it turned me on. But because I had said it once, he believed he knew all there was to know about me, and I was too embarrassed to bring it up again. I was too embarrassed to say: No, it's not enough.

To say, I see you try, but in fact it's worse than nothing to see you make a plan to hold me in a certain way, to see you make a decision and execute what you think will work best for me.

I want you to want to do it. That's the only way. I want it to all be as fluid and natural as the movement of you swatting a fly, as baked into your physiology as a thing like that.

You hate me, I thought sometimes, when you see me drink or cry or cut myself, but you don't hate me in the right way.

Your disgust is domesticated. I fear that your distaste is that of your average husband – not the glittering and sexual kind you used to show me when you looked down at me, before I won you.

2019, Athens

Maybe the thing I fear most of all is losing sex. Sex is so wonderful because it is one of the few things in adult life which can completely take you out of yourself. There is a pure singularity to it which leaves no room for your ordinary mind. All the things I love most – sex, romance, drinking – are like that.

I know what I want should count. What I desire ought to be as important as what you think when you look at me, but all the things which excite me, which make me as physical and voracious and forceful as a man, are to do with things being done to me. Always things are being done to me. Rarely do I do things myself.

When I was younger and still believed myself to be hideous, I used to think of my body as one that men liked to sleep with, but not to look at. I willed this into truth by never letting them look at me. I made love in the dark and covered myself afterwards, clumsy and childlike, so that they really did never look at me.

Once I told this theory of mine to a man named Luca when I was seventeen on a trip to Berlin. He was older, in his mid twenties, and part of the group I was holidaying with. I didn't know him as well as I did the others and was attracted by his arrogant smirk and casual dismissals of things not to his taste, whether that was a book or a person or a food. We were drunk and sitting on a kerb in Kreuzberg after a bar shut and I told him my feelings in a foolish gush of earnestness. He seemed sympathetic and said mild, comforting things in response.

Even later, when we had all been ejected from another club, our friend Sophie was talking about her yoga practice and how fit and strong she had become, when Luca turned to me and said, 'Perhaps you should take that up too,' and smiled slowly and the casual cruelty stunned me so much that I cried into my paper cup of vodka.

I walked shakily away from the group, wandering until I found a patch of grass to collapse down on and wallow in my absurd misery. An old weathered woman wearing several coats in the warm July dawn came and sat with me and offered to share her booze. 'Is it a man?' she asked, and I nodded, although it wasn't the kind of trouble she must have thought it was. The next night, predictably, Luca and I slept together.

I made mistakes like that all the time, seeking affirmation from the very worst people, so that what I must have been after deep down was confirmation of the fears instead of their dismissals. Luca and others confirmed for me that I truly was a thing built for use and base pleasure – but not to be looked at with pleasure, not to be beautiful or pristine. And so sex was what I could count on, a definite expression of my purpose. I learned to like that well enough to make up for the lack of beauty – learned to love it, rely on it enough to make my navigation of the places I went and lived in feel safe and fun.

Sometimes that skill slipped away from me without warning. I gained a lot of weight very quickly while in the middle of some crisis, maybe, so that none of my clothes fit and I walked around hunched over and frightened. Not infrequently I suffered inexplicable allergy flare-ups, which would make the skin on my face explode into strange and unsightly red welts around my eyes and mouth. They made me look diseased and haggard, twenty years older than I was. Walking around Dublin when that happened was a kind of hell, all my reliable tricks undone in an instant. A man would begin to size up my body and then recoil when he arrived to the face. It cut into me so much I could barely function and sometimes didn't, taking to my bed until I could pass for more or less good-looking again.

I don't know who to be without sex. I don't know how to access the ways of being which bring me relief and joy. Everything which does is bound up in sex somehow. The songs I listen to, all attached to someone I've been obsessed with. The films which break my heart, huge gorgeous eyes flooding the screen, showing impossible dynamics, passion which goes on and on and never ends because it can always be rewound.

And most of all, the feeling of walking around a foreign city: off an airbus in a short dress and sunglasses, a hopeful prayer for adventure pranging in my chest, feeling seen, made real anew by all the people who look with admiration or curiosity; those exchanges making it seem as though I could be anyone at all, begin new stories, live a thousand lives.

13

Once, when I was a child of eight or nine, I came downstairs in the night, confused from dreaming and looking for water. When I opened the kitchen door, lit up in the hallway half-light was a girlfriend of my father's who had fallen asleep there at the table with a cigarette in her hand. Her dressing gown had fallen open and I could see her small breasts slack against her chest and was frightened by the sight.

I thought of her at strange times over the years – there were a dozen or so childhood images like that one, of partners of one or other of my parents, moments I was too young to understand or contextualise and so they stuck with me (the French pastry chef who emerged grinning from the bathroom with his dick flopping out of his boxers, whispering something I can't remember).

The girlfriend hadn't been ugly or old, she didn't disturb me because she was decrepit. She was attractive and slim and buoyant in waking life, and this night remained with me only because it was a sight which taught me that a woman's nudity was not always erotic, not even always pleasant, was, indeed, at times pathetic to behold.

14

One evening near Christmas, having left his computer at work, Ciaran asked to use mine to send some emails. I realised afterwards he had not logged out, and then remembered standing in his kitchen at dawn in that time which felt so long ago, reading the endless, desperate, adoring message from Freja.

I felt sick with the sudden surge of power and possibility I had before me. There was no time limit. I could look at every single thing he had ever said about me, or ever said to her. I could see, finally, how their Christmas reconciliation and subsequent split came about, what he was thinking when he came back to me, whether he truly wanted to.

For days afterwards I pored through them at any spare moment I could find in work. My nausea rose. I felt myself filling up with his minutiae. I was engorged with him like an insect fat with blood.

But it was all so much nothing, so much nothing I did not already know.

This invasion was filthier than my first because of its sheer mundanity. At least then there had been something to be legitimately scandalised by.

Now, I was bored. There were cruel parts, certainly, parts hard to stomach: her cloying attempts to undermine me and my looks; his feverish need to keep reassuring her that I was only temporary, nothing real, nothing like her.

So what? I thought, scrolling.

I needed more, to be hurt more. I wanted to see that they continued to cheat, that they were planning to run away together, that they wanted to kill me.

I wanted lists of every flaw in my body, every way in which I was laughable and the object of their amused pity.

It was all so ordinary and underwhelming. They were just two idiots in a mess, who kept convincing and then un-convincing one another of things. They weren't star-crossed, just dithering, dependent people who couldn't stay away from each other because they hadn't worked out how to imagine anything different.

I had given up so much to be a part of this drama and I saw now how bad the part, how shoddy the script.

I kept looking, to find something, to justify the looking, until I arrived all the way back to years earlier, before I had met him. He had sent her a photograph he had taken of the two of them in bed, him kneeling over her and holding his dick above her plump, bare vagina. I looked, horribly compelled, and then logged out quickly and deleted his account from my computer.

That night I dreamed that I was him fucking Freja. I had dreamed of sleeping with her before, or of watching him do it, but in the dream I was him, full of him, full up with him, it was my dick stiff and purple brushing against her.

From then on I would never be really jealous of her again. The feelings would still be there somewhere, when he talked about her or I saw her online, but just as reflex. They were at a remove, not a part of my real self any more. It was as though I had been struck with a belt for years, and suddenly my flesh was replaced with something else, something inanimate. The pain was still going on, but it was no longer happening to me, it was happening to a statue.

January 2014

1

Once a year after Christmas Ciaran visited his father Peter where he lived near the Wicklow Mountains.

He had left his small family in Denmark when Ciaran was seven years old. Every few years after that he would reappear in Copenhagen, wild-haired, weathered, spiteful, drunk, and take his son to dinner.

The older he became, the more Ciaran grew to hate the emptiness of this occasional gesture and to hate Peter himself. And perhaps sensing the growing animosity from the beautiful brittle teenage boy sitting opposite him, Peter in turn grew hard and jeering.

I went with Ciaran to visit in the January of 2014, leaving Waterford where I had spent Christmas. We took a train and then a bus and then a cab to where he lived, a barely inhabitable rented cottage, freezing and mucky and mouldy. He had been there a number of years by the time I visited, so his routine was embedded in the dirt of the place. He had his cafetière and his stove kept clean, and a desk where he wrote endless unpublished letters to newspapers about unacceptable failures in local roads and services. Everything else he ignored.

It was something to see the old man come up against Ciaran. His features were handsome still, though brutally boiled looking, all of him purple and mottled. It seemed to me as though he must have waited all year, conserving energy in his little cave, so that he would have the strength to destroy his son. There was no action so meaningless that it could not be mocked with the manic acceleration of an insane stand-up comedian. I watched him do impressions of the sissy way Ciaran smoked a cigarette for so long that veins sprang dangerously from his temples, livid patches spreading on his cheeks.

He served us dinner, mashed potatoes and supermarket chicken Kiev, and we ate it off our knees gathered round the fireplace. Ciaran told some banal anecdote about work, about a gallery running out of wine and bringing out instead some elderly cans of Druid Cider from a back room, and while he told it he was animated, his wrists rolled slightly in the somewhat camp manner that he had when excited. Peter set his plate down on the dirty floor and leaned forward from his seat by the fire, rotating his wrists and bowing his head down near his knees, let his tongue loll out of his mouth grotesquely – and then sprang back upright and laughed, catching my eye.

But still Ciaran smiled and dragged a fork through his mashed potatoes. Still he would not break. This was a bargain they had struck – his father could let all of his poison and madness out on him, but Ciaran would not cry, would not raise his voice, would not storm out. He would bear it, and by bearing it could punish him. He was so superhumanly able to be still that there would never be any release for his father, no conclusion to the pain. This was how they came to know each other in adulthood.

They were not similar men in superficial ways. Ciaran was disgusted by Peter: that his old clothes and half-rotten boots smelled of mildew, that his meals came largely from tins or ready-meal packages, that empty bottles were strewn about his house with no humility, no shame. But I looked at them sitting there that evening, enduring each other in the flickering light, and was startled by their identical expressions.

Decades of resentment and things unsaid had calcified and left them paralysed in matching sneers. There was no way, now, that they could ever say that they loved one another, having never said it to begin with, but they were incapable too of naming their hatred. There may have been a time once when Ciaran was capable of saying, 'I hate you for leaving me, for leaving me alone when I was a child,' but if such a time had existed it had long since passed.

And if Peter had ever been inclined to look his boy straight in the eye and say that he was sorry, that he had been young himself then and unsure, unstable – if he had ever wanted to reach out and steady Ciaran's hand, the one that constantly worried the threads of his sleeve when he was with his father, if he had ever wanted to take that hand and say, 'When I left you it didn't make me happy. There was no pleasure in my life after I left. It was only that I didn't know how to take care of you, but I wish I did know. I wish I'd known then, and I wish I knew now.'

If he had ever wanted to slip his arms under Ciaran's and hold him close, and say, 'I am your father. Nothing will ever change that. I didn't just help make you – there is a part of me which you made when you were born, and which will always be yours.'

If he had wanted to do any of that – well, it was too late.

When my own dad was a small child, he had a schoolmate whose father died, and he became convinced that his own father would shortly go the same way. He would sit at the bottom of their road at the end of the day, a newly built estate for a newly ascending working class, waiting for his father to come home from work. He gnawed on his little hands and pulled at the sleeve of his prickly school jumper, praying anxiously for the moment the big man would round

191

the corner and smile his big devastating grin and hoist him up back home.

When I was a similar age as Dad was then, I sang in a church choir, treasuring my occasional solos and shutting my eyes piously during the best hymns, still a believer. One evening I was expecting my dad to be there, I had a whole verse to myself, and grew increasingly panicked as the mass went on and I could not see him. Soon I began to cry silently up there in the choir, keeping my eyes as wide open as I could so that the people down there wouldn't see. My tears streamed throughout my solo and then the mass was over and I cried properly, balling up my fists and digging them into my sockets and doubling over, certain – but certain – he had died.

Then he ran to me, having been there all that time, having only been delayed by traffic, he took me in his arms as he told me over and over again he had been there all that time, even though I couldn't see him.

How lucky I have been that so much of my pain is from fearing the loss of what I already have, instead of suffering the absence entirely, as Ciaran did.

2

The annual staff party came around in March and I wanted to drink. I had kept my drinking more or less moderate, to a degree that prevented Ciaran from doing anything but irritably glancing at me.

I had been good for a long time. Now, the feeling I used to regularly have before I met him, the restless and soaring need for a big messy night, was back and it seemed to have been growing privately all that time.

In the days leading up to the party I bought a new dress made of a clingy grey material which knotted in the middle and had cut-outs which framed the soft neat curve where my waist became my hips. I bought new make-up and experimented with it alone before he arrived back in the evenings. I cut down on food so I would feel light and powerful.

In a big anonymous club on Harcourt Street, forty of us assembled after work. I had got ready in the bathrooms with some of the other younger women, and they all gawked and whooped at my outfit, halfway between admiration and mockery. I was overdressed. I was dressed as I would have been in the before days, when I was going to the party of a well-known DJ, or the gig of someone I was trying to sleep with. My body spilt out of its dress generously and sexually, my heels were high, my make-up polished and harsh. I soaked up their attention, hoping they envied me, wanting to eat that up, the brief thrill of feeling better than them.

In the club I drank glasses of frosty Pinot Grigio in no time at all, pounding them back and then wandering idly to another counter, another group of people, to get my next. I talked to people I never usually talked to, surprised myself and them by being funny and personable and interested in what they had to say. Nothing works like drinking does.

By the time it was ten and all the bosses had left I was entering the stage of pure hunger, pure need. My heart rate quick and joyful, my conversation unthinking and unending. I smoked constantly and moved on to spirits, moved into that place where what you want is clear and foul-tasting things, want bitter powder that burns the back of your throat like bleach, where you are total want.

A man I'd never spoken to before who worked in the IT department sidled behind me as I danced and put his hands on my waist where the cut-outs were. I jumped and turned to face him and laughed and shook him off. He was short and pink and sweaty, twenty years older than me. His hair shone with gel.

'Don't you have a boyfriend?' he asked me.

'Yes,' I replied, startled.

He leaned in and whispered in my ear, 'Well, how the fuck did he let you out like this?' And then he trailed his awful hand down my backside and roughly squeezed me and then let go and glided away quickly before I could shriek or push him off.

I walked home later, the fifteen minutes up Rathmines Road, which took me much longer because of my shoes. As I went I thought, over and over again, *How the fuck did he let you out like this? How the fuck did he let you out like this? How the fuck did he let you out like this?*

Trying to puzzle it apart, find its meaning and why it had stopped me cold.

When I arrived home I was much later than I said I would be, and Ciaran was up, and I must have been acting strangely because he screamed at me and demanded that I account for my time and accused me of having been with another man, which he had never done before.

I laughed and he grabbed my wrist and banged it against our kitchen table and I thought, *Break it, why don't you? Do something. How the fuck did you let me out like this?*

Then he recovered and remembered that the way to hurt me is to ignore me. He left and went to our bedroom, and I locked myself in the bathroom and lifted up the sexy new dress and masturbated, quickly and shamefully, thinking about the ugly man who had touched me at the party, the way he had confirmed that Ciaran owned me. And then, just at the end as I was starting to come, I thought of Ciaran accusing me of being with another man.

It was the first time I had conceived of being with anyone but him since we met. I gasped, grabbed the sink.

2019, Athens

For someone I love to prefer another woman to me, to choose her body over mine even in the abstract, was once the most vile experience I could imagine. I could not bear to watch a film with Ciaran sometimes – wasn't able to relax for the two hours in which he was seeing a person who was better to look at than me. I clawed my thighs slowly and deeply beneath the duvet. In my head I swore off sugar, milk, bread, anything that might nourish me. I vowed to wake at five a.m. and do sit-ups until I couldn't breathe.

I think that my easy offering of myself to others is a way to dispute this pain, to fight with myself. Who cared what anyone did, if I could do this? If I could disregard myself first, then what did it matter if he did too?

I hate to write that, to put my facts in the hands of people who will sneer and feel annoyed by their tawdry debasement.

Those who have been betrayed themselves, who cannot imagine cheating, who think of it as a crime that should be punishable by law, as some friends of mine do, will find it a self-serving and pathetic excuse for my infidelities.

There are those of you, the enlightened readers, who will find my willing debasement embarrassing. You will say that my choices are my own and should not be refracted through the lens of my need for men and their approval. They believe that any sexual greed is only my right and should be embraced, that I should simply extricate myself from monogamy, from stern boyfriends and their paternal domination, that I should wallow in my incontinent sexuality and enjoy it without shame.

But both things can be true.

True, yes, that I love to have sex, and that my love of it is not only about the act but about the multitude. I love the sex of knowing someone very well for years and just what will make them crumble and break open, but I also love to have sex with new people for not much more than their newness. I wish, when I leave them, that I could stay and sleep with them a hundred more times until I've exhausted all their strangeness, but I know too that the fact I can't is what makes the meeting so sacred.

Those moments have been the rawest, most tender flaying of myself, a return to the simplicity of what I know to be more or less the point of life, of coming together with another person without care for what the next day will bring, unexpected connection without fear.

True also, though, that despite my often sincerely shameless enjoyment of sexual greed, my promiscuity has sometimes been compelled by self-loathing. By a sudden and desperate need to have my beauty confirmed, because I missed a man and wanted to take revenge on him and on myself for losing him, because I wanted to throw away a good boyfriend I didn't feel I deserved.

Tedious, I know, to say such things. People talk more and more about female desire nowadays, which we all agree is good, is a step forward. But I am amazed to hear critics upset at any hint that woman's desire may still be authored in some way by men.

We should, after all, have our own desires, free of men!

Of course we should. I can only imagine; I would love to feel it. I would love to have one moment of want in my life when I am sure what I'm feeling is all my own and nothing to do with men, with what has happened with men in the past, with what they have said about me and my body, what thoughts they have put in my head without me even knowing.

It doesn't mean that I blame them very much, or excuse myself from blame. Why do I have to call them bad, and myself good, to simply observe what takes place in the world? What power men have had over me seems more like a neutral fact than a reason for me to hate them. And who would I be to hate them anyway? Couldn't I have made myself immune to them with will and education and pride, in this late century, couldn't I have had some other great love in my life than for them?

Of course I could, but I did not, and this, my story, is the story of that failure.

3

Ciaran flew to Copenhagen to visit his mother in April. I unravelled in the apartment, alone at last. I mixed tequila with soda and lime and sat on the couch drinking and smoking from six until midnight.

I leafed furiously through glossy women's magazines, always with one hand on the internet, checking, scrolling, refreshing. There was not a single night I did not go to bed shitfaced.

My mind was a flapping, beating thing, never still. I realised in his absence that I had become used to killing this feeling with whatever Ciaran was doing at the time, whether that was fucking me or ignoring me or sneering at me. The hysteria, the upset was bad, but its absence was – was. It was absence. It was the great nothing of my heart, my own boundless greed and inability to be sated reflected back at me.

It was a stroke of luck that I had chosen someone so aloof, so in love with another woman.

Maybe I had even chosen him because of it, because he so resisted loving me.

But it wouldn't have mattered in the end.

Whatever he offered me would never have sufficed.

I had chosen someone who was by nature indifferent, and made it my project to make him love me.

It had seemed impossible, but I had made it happen in the end.

I realised this when he was gone. He called me and told me he missed me.

'I want to be in bed with you,' he said, and I could hear the smile in his voice and was startled by its fondness and lack of guile.

How had I done it, broken down this man who seemed so like a statue, so unmoving and perfect? I marvelled at my own power.

People said that you had to be yourself, and be strong and independent to be in love.

They said that meekness and submission would only drive men away, that confidence was attractive. But I had done it, had worn him down with weakness.

He did not love me – couldn't, for what Me was there to love? What Me had he ever known? – but he had become attached to me, dependent on me.

I had carefully created a circumstance in which a kind of love could be bred in him, like a scientist manipulating lab conditions.

I had exhausted his reserves, eroded his natural resistance, and now I was finished.

May 2014

1

At first I wrote my frustrations only to myself. I allowed myself to say to my diary, cautiously, that it was difficult to be with Ciaran, with a person so negative and lacking in affection.

Then, every few weeks, there would be some man who caught my eye in a particular way, made me feel vibrantly, visibly sexual. I had not felt bold this way in so long, and it came back to me how much I loved the brazen public nature of it.

I stood on a tram gripping a handrail and looked up to see an attractively wealthy-looking man in an olive overcoat staring at me and I looked back just as boldly and for the rest of the journey we caught eyes again and again.

When not looking directly at him I still presented myself to him, moving my lips, wetting them in a way that could just about be plausibly natural. My whole body was flush with the heat of it, between my legs bright with feeling.

I wrote these incidents down. I wrote, timidly at first, and then with growing abandon, the kinds of things I would have liked the men to do to me. My diary became a valve. I got home from work and still I cooked our meals and asked how his day was, but would be looking forward already to when that was over and I could be alone with my thoughts. I wondered if he noticed that I no longer persisted when he ignored me or was spiteful, that I did not cry or panic or lock myself in the bathroom any more.

We slept together less and less, but gradually enough that it was only cause for him to occasionally grumble, could be put down to the natural waning of long-term desire. He seemed not to notice that anything was really different in me.

I still believed that I loved him. The love was so real to me. I wrote in my diaries about it. I blamed myself for what was wrong between us, my sexual wantonness and greed. I loved him, I wrote, but he wasn't satisfying me sexually. I loved him, I wrote, but he just didn't like the same things as I did. I needed to explore. I needed to experiment – but that didn't mean I didn't love him!

I still so believed in love, even then. I needed to cast myself as a slut with unshakeable proclivities to make any sense of the thing.

I thought often of how I had felt once, so strongly and clearly, that I would never hurt him. I was determined then to be nothing like Freja.

(I tried not to think, reproachfully, that perhaps his girl-friends cheated on him because of his penetrating coldness; but think it I did, and with balmy relief.)

'He can never find out,' I wrote, 'beautiful Ciaran, the most beautiful man in the world. I can't confirm his suspicions that everyone – but especially women – that everyone is essentially bad. Although I suppose I am proving him right by what I'm doing.'

My mind was splitting once more.

2

In June, a phone call from my father: he was in hospital in Waterford. There was a swelling in his throat, which was affecting his swallowing and breathing. They had taken him to do a biopsy of the tissue obstructing, but had become so concerned by his breathing that they had kept him in.

We hadn't spoken in a few weeks. His beloved aunt had died the previous year and I had made an excuse not to go to the funeral. Things had been cordially frosty between us since then. I remember that the funeral took place during a week when my relationship with Ciaran was especially bad and I did not feel that I could leave in the middle of that. I needed to stay to keep watch over the badness, keep its embers tidy and undangerous. I preferred to stay and fight with Ciaran than to go home and be with my family.

My father couldn't understand why. I blamed it on work, but he knew my job was perfunctory, a place to turn up late and watch the clock. The journey was so short, was the thing. The journey would only have been two hours in the car; he would have come for me.

It was difficult to lie to my father. He knew when I was lying but couldn't bring himself to say so outright. He knew that I lied to convince myself that my messes could be overwritten. And this must have made the lies all the more jarring for him to hear, covering up things he could have no grasp on.

3

After my father's call I arranged to take time off work to go and visit him. I sat at my desk, emailing my manager and booking tickets. I let Ciaran know that I was going, not asking him to come with me.

I felt sure that Dad was going to die. A punishment, I thought.

A punishment for ignoring my family; a punishment for needing only someone who could not see me, instead of needing the people who could.

I had loved my father so fiercely for my entire life.

Through all the squalid mess of my teenage years and beyond, during the very worst things, we had always stayed close, I had always needed him. It was only with Ciaran that I had changed, and now the punishment for that would come, the thing I had feared most all my life.

I was gripped by a sudden awareness of how terribly alone I was. My father was one of the few anchors I had to myself. When I didn't know who I was at a given moment I could think of him and count the years back to the start. When I didn't know who I was I could at least think of him and say, *I am his*. Without him, would I be forced to be this new person, this Ciaran's-person for the rest of my life? What would hold me down any more, what would make me real? I felt that I would simply float away, that there would be nothing left of the thing I called Me before Ciaran.

I tapped my limbs and hummed tunelessly the whole journey down, buzzing with anxiety; I needed to see my father. If I saw him before anything happened then things would be OK. Just as when, years ago, Ciaran had left me I had been consumed by the feeling that things would turn out all right if I could only make him answer his phone or look me in the eye. My huge, ridiculous ego – the belief that I could stop and start the world with my presence.

When I found his room, he smiled at me and I burst into tears and ran to kneel beside him and grasp his hand saying, 'Dad, Dad, Dad.' He didn't look ill, but he looked old. His eyes were as warm and bright as ever but there were new lines. His hair was all white now, and soft and thin like a baby's. So much time had passed. So much time had passed since I had thought clearly about anything but Ciaran.

He laughed at my histrionics and patted my back in the same tender awkward way we had always showed physical affection to each other.

'Everything's OK,' he said. 'And if it's not, we'll take care of it and then it will be.' He spoke slowly, painfully.

I cried, not because I didn't believe him, but because I did.

I had so missed listening to him say this thing, this thing he had always said to me throughout my life, in a million different ways. He had always said it, and I had always listened, always believed it, no matter how terrible the thing I was enduring. But I hadn't heard it in years now, had not cared to listen for it, and I cried because I was ashamed and for all the other things I had been deaf to, the sounds like this I would never get back. My dad was always able to save me from anything, no matter how reckless or inexplicable, he was always able to save me from anything but myself.

4

That evening, having been assured by my father and his doctor that nothing bad had actually happened yet, and that nothing at all would change overnight, I was restless and fidgety, unable to sit still or to be alone with my mind. I needed to see somebody, and went into the city to find my ex-boyfriend Reuben.

Reuben was my first love. We had met when I was fifteen and he was seventeen, fallen in a helpless, unfairly incomparable love. Until I met Ciaran, every boy and man I knew was measured against him and left badly wanting. Physically, he was the only real precursor to Ciaran.

We met at a techno night – an inordinately popular genre of music in Waterford – and were a couple a week later. He was long and angular and thin like Ciaran, but golden and dark instead of pale and blond. His eyes were a soft and clear light brown, like a cartoon woodland animal's. He was only seventeen but seemed much older than me. He had three tattoos and was already in university, having skipped two years.

When we met I was a virgin, and nervous of sex. I had briefly dated boys before him, boys I had liked very much but who had shoved their hands down my pants or into my shirts with no warning or finesse. I had pushed them away and they had left me because of it.

Reuben and I wrote letters to each other when he was in university in Dublin and I was home, during the week. We wrote five pages of A4 refill pad, back and forth, every week. They were filled with lyrics, bits of poems, little drawings, as well as everything we were doing and feeling. It was the first time I was open in this way, outside of my diary.

I wrote poetry at the time, and won some prizes. The poems were good, sometimes because of a genuine candour, and often because I was not yet worldly enough to know to avoid plagiarism of theme and style. One poem I wrote about Reuben won a prize, and I flushed reading it aloud in a children's library, because it was so intimate and bodily. His was the first body I knew and I loved it deeply. It was the first time I loved a man's body, and the only time that love was not somehow dark or convoluted or ruined. We never had sex.

He was shy, reluctant or unable to name what we had together. That didn't matter – it was as true and obvious as the fact of our bodies. On Valentine's Day he gave me a card, in the square where we met with our friends most weekends to stand and smoke and drink coffee and swap CDs.

'Don't read it now,' he said, and kissed me. I tore the envelope as soon as he was out of sight and read it hurriedly.

'I'm excited we will both be on holidays soon,' he wrote, 'so that I can see you all the time. I love you.'

It was the first time a boy had said those words to me. I remember them clearly because I did something so cartoonish when I read them: I literally jumped for joy, right there in the street, in the middle of Waterford, with everyone watching.

We broke up six months later because of me. I was unhappy even then, even when I was blissfully happy with him. I was already deeply into my cutting and starving. I knew enough to keep that hidden from him at first, and then I slowly forgot. I began to confide in him how I felt, my inability to function, what I was driven to do to myself.

It upset him. He was harsh with me – harsh for him, anyway.

'You can't complain about feeling bad, about being depressed, if you aren't trying to sleep, trying to eat, trying to care about yourself.'

I found this outrageous. I was shocked that he was not impressed and cowed by my delicacy, as other boys had been. Why did he not find my frail, picturesque sadness alluring? I think now this was my first and most serious mistake – not listening to that advice. He was just a teenager, wasn't right about everything or even most things, but he was right about that.

I was wallowing in the glamour of my sadness. I read an article in *Vogue* around that time which said something like: 'This season's looks lean towards Gothic drapery, knee socks and heavy eyeliner, showing something that every teenage girl knows: that sadness can be a kind of beauty.'

We kept on, for a while, after that, but it was over for me. I broke up with him almost a year to the day that we had got together. We saw each other a handful of times after that, after he'd moved to England, around Christmas or in summer.

There was never bad blood. We never once met up without crying and kissing. He became a sort of touchstone for me, as the rest of my life spiralled out of control. Once when I was nineteen we met and kissed and cried as usual and told each other that we loved each other.

'Let's stop messing around,' I said. 'We love each other. I made a mistake before. Let's just be together properly.'

He agreed, and then I got the bus back to Dublin and we never spoke of it again. But it was enough, or almost, to know that he was alive and that he loved me.

5

We met in the square as it was becoming evening. He looked good, a little broader in the shoulders, had a swimmer's body now, had joined a team when he moved to Montreal to do his fellowship.

He was tanned and had more tattoos than before, looked like somebody I would have seen and coveted in a magazine, in *NME* or *Vice*, when I was younger. He looked like someone I would have chosen as an example of the future I wanted for myself. His lean bicycle and lean self and the earring and the ease in his body.

He smiled up at me from the bench and I was amazed, as I always was when I saw him again, to feel no differently towards him than when we first met. It always felt like a sleight of hand, a bit of magic, that we both still liked each other so much, that nothing had ever ruined things for us definitively. I felt so much myself with Reuben, so rooted still.

Was it the lack of sex that did it? It was hard not to think that, like the girls in *Halloween*, it was only the sex that doomed me; hard not to think that I might have got on all right without it. I could have been the Final Girl.

We went to a pub and huddled in a corner, sitting close together to hear one another over the noise of the ceilidh band playing. I told him about my father, about Ciaran, told him more about the reality of Ciaran than I had anyone but my diary.

I heard myself speeding through the whole story, making a meal of all the ways that Ciaran had wronged me, skimming over my own transgressions, my willing compliance. I didn't mention more recent developments, my thwarted rages, the sexual adventuring I was doing in my head more and more now.

I tried to point him towards how healthy I was, how I ate so well and even tried to exercise a little. I told him how I always slept a full night, not mentioning that the teenage insomnia he had known had mutated into a kind of sleeping sickness, that I could sleep for twelve or more hours now, and would if left alone.

It was late and we were drunk, holding hands.

'This is so you,' Reuben said.

'What is?'

'You always think your pain is the most painful. You always think it's uniquely awful.'

I stared back at him mutely (even then aware of how my face became prettier in vacancy, even then parting my lips and sweetly widening my eyes in surprise).

He laughed. 'It's fine. I'm not giving out. I know you; I know this is what you're like. It's just – you've barely asked about me. You have no idea what's going on in my life. You never really have.'

'Tell me,' I said, face moving closer.

'No! I'm not going to list all the things wrong with my life so you can take them in and then compare them to yourself.'

It was bad, what he was saying, and true, but he was smiling as well.

'I don't know how you get away with it,' he said, still smiling and shaking his head, and then I kissed him.

2019, Athens

I see beautiful teenage boys now and my heart bends at their broad shoulders and neat torsos, the golden triangle, at their tanned long calves and miraculous forearms. I hunger in their direction just like the men I disdain for doing the same to girls. I can't help viewing these boys in the same way I did when I was a teenager, I see the ones who would have obsessed me, and guess at which ones would have felt the same about me.

Strange to know you'll never again be with the kind of person who made you love first, their imprint inescapable. There are just a few portals backward, if you don't plan to become predatory – the boys you loved back then, grown now, but the teenager still visible within, to you at least. With them and only them, you can feel yourself as rapt and opened up and simple as you once were, both of you as beautiful as children to each other.

Nobody who loves me from now on will ever know, really know, really believe, that I was a beautiful child once.

6

I stayed at home for three more nights after the biopsy had been taken. I googled my father's symptoms relentlessly, and found a million people saying it was nothing and another million saying it was terminal.

When I slept with Reuben in his old room it was like sleeping with a wonderful ghost. I touched him in places I had forgotten and then remembered them in an instant. I touched new parts of him, places I hadn't when we were young but which still felt familiar.

At first I froze when he touched me, afraid I wasn't as lithe and slight as I had been when we'd known each other, but under his hands my body felt reversed, pliable and unused again. I felt virginal, felt that we could correct a decade of wrongs together.

He trailed his hands over my ribs and stomach and I didn't breathe in, as I instinctively did still with Ciaran to make myself thinner.

Nothing was dramatic. It was soft and easy. It was almost funny: we both laughed. It was like the feeling of talking late at night after the light had been turned off and trying not to let your laughter run away with you.

It was amazing how different it was to sleeping with Ciaran. Part of what had made me addicted to Ciaran's body and to having sex with him was the quality of my need. It was acute, desperate, anguished. It was trying to win an argument.

It wanted him to surrender to me, either to become totally loving, totally mine, or to play dominant in an overt and quantifiable way. But he just existed, passive and removed, fucking me in a way that reminded me of necessary tasks, of the way he ate – not without any pleasure, but even so, with a heavy sense of function. I could never get any closer to him, could never satisfy myself. And that made me want him more for years, had made me wild with violent need.

Now, without it, I could feel the silliness of sex for the first time in forever. It wasn't cinematic or beautiful. I could feel my body once more and it did not feel unfinished, as it always did with Ciaran. It did not feel like something that had been forgotten about in the middle of creation, did not feel like a hasty sketch without the proper lines put in. It didn't feel in wait.

I felt it slide, slick and friendly, against Reuben's and the flesh didn't seem spare but instead put to good use. I filled his hands, made him happy. I was surprised by my voracity, surprised at all the things I wanted to do to him and the shamelessness with which I asked for his permission to do them. He was beautiful, and he was my friend, and I wanted him so much, and he was not Ciaran.

I felt no guilt that night.

We woke the next morning, his breath was sweet and milky, even first thing, like a kid's. We grinned at one another sheepishly and kissed and stretched about yawning in bed, hoping his parents had left the house. I didn't try to say this time that we were in love and should be together.

We didn't need to talk about anything. It was perfect – he was going back to Montreal, and I had my own foreign

216

land to return to. I was keeping the secret of Ciaran from myself, storing him with demented precision just outside my active thoughts. I could feel him there, waiting to erupt and ruin the calm glow of my morning with Reuben, but I kept him at bay.

Had to return to I was hopping and swearing at it, furniture upside the doorstep, and with a mind of... section on tip-toe... progress progress and run among I rubbed humming and among ... the condign ray and read the corruption of me... morning with Reuben and I... I was... at bay.

7

When I left Reuben's house, walking to the hospital to say goodbye to my father, a surge of adrenalin crested through me.

I walked faster and harder and concentrated on my father, what I wanted to ask his doctor, trying to use all the panic up on that. Near the Ardkeen Road I broke into a ragged jog – how Ciaran would have rolled his eyes to see me gasp, my slobby technique! – and began to shake my head violently from side to side when an intrusive thought came, the idea of me putting my key in the door, of him looking at me, the idea of him knowing what I had done, him smelling it on me even without a sense of smell, knowing in an instant that I was disgusting, that he had been right all along to think me unworthy of him.

I shook my head, rattling my brain, blurring my vision, and when that didn't work I bent down on the side of the motorway and closed my eyes and pressed my thumbs into the recesses of the sockets, and drove my knuckles into my temples hard, letting me see only flashing blobs of white and dark, flooding my vision, saturating me entirely.

In the hospital my dad was listlessly eating and it moved me to see his boredom. I sat with him for a few hours, watching news programmes and quiz shows and chatting about this and that. He asked what I was reading and I could not remember the last book I had read so instead recounted an opinion of a novel I had gathered from a Sunday supplement. His voice sounded clearer than it had the day before. I wanted to be touching him, to have my arms around him or to lie in the bed beside him but there was no way to do these things.

On the bus back to Dublin I travelled in a state of prayer. I bargained and pleaded. I would give up drinking, food, pleasure. I would stop daydreaming about sex with strangers, stop writing sordid thoughts in my diary. I would relent, go back to being whatever had made him capitulate in the first place.

And then my father couldn't die and Ciaran couldn't leave me.

Ciaran would never have to suffer through finding out what I was really like – so desperate to be filled up, to be of use, to please.

I would be small and safe and dry and quiet. I would learn humility and true meekness, not just the performance of them.

8

When I got in that evening I greeted him and curled up beside him on the sofa where he sat typing in pyjamas and glasses. His hair was a little long and the loose curls smelled like sour sweat and I breathed them in. I threw my bag and coat on the ground, as though completely exhausted, and pulled a blanket over me.

He asked how my dad was and I told him we wouldn't know for a while. I rested my head on his shoulder as my heart hammered in my chest, wondering if my voice sounded different, if there was some hair or mark of Reuben's on me somewhere which could give me away.

Later in the bathroom I saw that a small bruise dappled my thigh, and though it could have come from anywhere, I cut right through it with a small kitchen knife, filled briefly with the mad and pure decisiveness of a teenager once more. I would have carved his name all over me if I could have, if I thought it would make him happy.

I was home, and every mitigating thought had vanished. In Waterford I had tried to rationalise what I had done, telling myself that Reuben and I were such old news that it barely counted as infidelity, telling myself I was upset and needed comfort, I was drunk.

But back in Dublin – back in my familiar position, slumped on the tiles, head against the cistern, muffling sobs into my lap to avoid a fight – I knew the truth. I had done it because I wanted to do it. I had done it because I wanted someone who wasn't Ciaran, wanted someone whose affection and attention was straightforward. I wanted something easy to understand, and I understood Reuben and I understood fucking and I got what I wanted. Ciaran was going to lie in bed beside me, touch me, maybe even want to fuck me himself, not knowing that I was dirty, and a liar.

I didn't understand how I had lied about so many things when they all felt true at the time. I loved him so much, no other love had ever felt as stingingly clean as the one I felt for him. I had meant it when I said that I wanted more than anything never to hurt him, to help him be able to trust people again.

Even that, I supposed, had been a lie – I hadn't wanted him to trust people, I'd wanted him to trust me, only me. I wanted to be the one who could shatter his outside and get to the good parts, wanted to be the saint who made him see it wasn't all women who were sluts and liars; or maybe to make him see that it was all of them, except for me, only me, and I was the only one he needed.

But now I'd done it, now I'd fucked it up. No matter how sweet Reuben and I were, and how innocent the quality of our ancient romance, the physical facts were plain. I had let another man kiss and touch and bend and fuck me, and were Ciaran to know these facts he would despise and leave me. I cried harder, biting down on my wrist to shut myself up, my brain a livid and impotent blaze.

After calming myself down I went to our bedroom and took out my computer. I blocked Reuben on every available platform and then on my phone too. My desperation had made me clear headed and cool. There was no strand between the two men except me. Nobody could ever tell him but me. He wouldn't find out. I just had to deal with it, put it away, and be good.

9

For one more month I did live this way, I pretended it had
never happened, that it was a thing that could be ignored.
I cooked dinner and stayed in and stopped drinking. I read
books and stopped watching garbage TV. On Friday nights
when he went out, I waited for him to come back, and did
nothing except wait. He seemed happy, as happy as he had
ever been. Having sex with him made me feel ill and
psychotic with splitting but I forced myself to do it anyway,
put it down as one more duty to make things safe again.

Then my father called in July, telling me he had got the
all-clear.

He would not only live, he hadn't been very sick at all.
Everything was fine.

That night I called Ciaran to tell him I would be home
late, and I went to a bar.

I drank wine on my own until I was drunk, and then I
went to a party, where I met a man I had known briefly
many years before. We kissed against the wall and then left
to find a hotel and fucked there all night, him pulling my
hair and slapping my face and grabbing my throat, me
urging him to keep doing it, asking him for more, more,
more.

10

In the morning Noah left to find his band and get back on the road, a ferry to catch and a gig in Liverpool that evening. He grinned his lopsided grin and told me he would be back in a few weeks and would call me then, ruffling my fringe and kissing my forehead as he went.

I showered in boiling water. My hair was a long matted mass from being tossed around with such casual abandon and I tore it into manageable segments, to soap it through and make it normal again. I scrubbed myself everywhere, especially inside. I was raw from the sex and made myself rawer with the cleaning. I had no idea what I would say to Ciaran when I returned home. My phone had died early the evening before.

I left, walking down Fitzwilliam Square.

I had been at a party in Portobello with Christina, already completely totalled, and had recognised Noah. He looked like an irresistibly attractive mess, handsome and chubby in a way that suggested pleasurable excess and partying, a chipped front tooth, mismatched clothes. He was something like a surfer gone wrong, with that long hair and the crinkled smile, and the laughing, knowing eyes. I saw him staring at me.

'Don't I know you?' I walked over and said.

He told me I was right, and I remembered then: we had met at a gig years before when he had played in a line-up with an ex-lover of mine.

'Are you still with that guy?' he asked, and I told him that I was not.

I kept trying to figure out what the exact moment was, the moment where I went from being convinced that I loved Ciaran and would do whatever it took to be with him, to standing swaying at a hotel reception at five a.m. with a near-stranger, giving it all up again, and again, and again.

11

I saw on my way home, checking my balance, that I had paid for the hotel – the whole lot of it, a week's wages for me, another little indignity to store away for later.

I had tried to do myself up as convincingly as possible, normal, pretty make-up, but I could feel myself sweating through it.

I had never been as afraid as I was that morning standing outside our apartment looking up at the window, seeing his books and cigarettes resting on the sill, knowing he was in there.

The moment I walked in I could see that everything had changed for us, for ever, already. Gone was the blank Ciaran, the cold Ciaran, the one who made me second-guess myself. He was frantic and red-eyed and shaking. He was shouting in a way that was almost crying.

I had been so worried about what I had done – the sex, the hotel – I had forgotten all about the fact that I had simply failed to come home.

'Where were you? Where the fuck were you?' he shouted in rising waves of indignation, grabbing my coat lapel and yanking on it.

'I'm so sorry,' I kept repeating, waiting for him to calm down, waiting to lie. I tried to touch his wrist soothingly and he pushed me away. I half fell, half sat on a kitchen chair.

'Are you still drunk?' he demanded, and I went to deny that I was before thinking better of it. I told him that I was. I told him that I was so relieved about my dad's news that I wanted to drink, that I had met Christina and we had had too much and gone back to her place and I'd just fallen asleep on the sofa.

He believed me. It was incredible the way he believed me. He was still so angry, but he was angry about the drinking and about the not coming home, about having worried him. He simply believed me, thought it was true just because I said it was. I marvelled that he who had lied to me for so long, about Freja and all of it, could assume I was telling the truth.

I got undressed and showered again, left him alone to come down from the shouting a little, and to clean myself more. When I finished and came back to the bedroom, he grabbed me and discarded my towel, lay me down on the bed.

'I'm sorry,' I said again and again as he kissed my neck and my hollow chest.

'I know,' he said, and kept going, insistent, although I was still and did not respond. His hands moved over me, touched me in the way he did when he wanted to have sex. I said nothing but did not move away. He put his fingers inside me, although I was not wet.

'I'm really tired,' I whispered, wriggling away. I didn't like to turn him down, but the alternative was worse. My body felt radioactive.

He smiled at me and lay my head down on the mound of pillows, arranged them, fanned my hair out so that I felt like a doll, or a corpse in repose. He knelt over me and kissed me gently on the forehead and, so slightly, in a way that could usually make me shiver, on the lips.

'I'm sorry,' I said again, and he shushed me. The way he was treating me would have made me so happy not long ago, the tenderness, the attention. It reminded me of a doctor's attention, firm and sure in that way. A few times a year I would go on my lunch break to give blood, just because I liked how careful they had to be with you, and that they'd touch you with such practised ease.

It was hurting me now, the attention. I wanted him to forgive me but to leave me alone, let me get some sleep, wake up and start again as though none of it had happened. I closed my eyes but he didn't stop. He kissed and stroked my neck again and began to move downwards.

'Please,' I said, and then, 'I don't want to' – a thing I'd never had to say before.

In the past he had turned away huffily at the merest hint of reluctance.

He knows, I thought, *on some level he must know that I've done something.*

'It's OK,' he said, still smiling down at me gently. 'You don't have to do anything. I'll do it. I'll make you feel better.'

And he went on kissing me, my breasts and my ribs. I prayed that the bruises that would surely appear had not appeared yet.

I tried one more time to stop it, turning to my side and huddling that way, saying, 'I – I –' Not able to construct a sentence that accounted for my distaste.

'It's OK.' He smiled again, as though I was just denying myself pleasure to be self-punitive, as though I needed to be reassured that I was allowed to enjoy this. He gently hooked an arm beneath my knee and prised my legs apart, and then he went down on me.

He held my hands down by my sides as he did so.

I rolled my eyes back in my skull as far as they would go, trying to get at the white light to block things out. I wanted to cry with repulsion, the idea of his mouth being where Noah's dick had been hours before. And yet I could not make him stop without telling him the truth, without

227

making him hate me. I could not bear the idea of him hating me. I was afraid of him, but I was selfish, too.

I counted in my head and when I thought I could, I faked an orgasm, stiffening the sinews in the softest part of my upper inner thigh, gasping and grabbing at his hand. I thrust myself towards him one, two, three times and then collapsed.

'Thank you,' I said, and had to hug him close to me for one more moment before I could turn over and pretend to sleep.

12

That was when it should have ended. It seems insane to me now that I somehow went on, but I believed still that I loved him and that the cheating was a symptom of my innate foulness. I didn't deserve love but I needed it.

The idea of telling him was simply beyond my imagination. The idea of willingly severing our domestic, daily devotions; the idea of having to get up in the morning without him. I could not picture it. It wasn't just that I dreaded it, I was genuinely unable to conceive of a world in which these things would take place.

I was in great pain, the lies and suppression, the smiles and fucking I had to fake. But I had lived with pain before. It would recede, I knew. A person can get used to anything.

Something else, too: I could not imagine reversing the narrative of us. I knew that I was bad, but nobody else did. With the telling, there would be a rewrite.

The way all of my friends secretly or not-so-secretly hated him, and thought he was bad for me. The fact that he had loved Freja, left me for her. His incredible coldness, the way his whole body could act as a refusal, facing away from me as I cried. The way he spoke to me, which left me feeling that I must be insane. All of these things would be different, re-cast. It would change everything, the telling, the badness inside me coming real.

August 2014

Noah and I messaged every day. I sent him pictures of my body and he made me laugh in a way I hadn't in for ever. One day in the office as we were chatting he told me to go to the bathroom and lock myself in a cubicle and masturbate thinking about what we had done in the hotel. I tucked my phone into my bra so my boss wouldn't see me carrying it out, and did as he told me. I came explosively, the thought of his lopsided grin looming over me, his dick in my mouth. I sent him a picture of my flushed face afterwards so he would know.

It felt almost like a safe game, a reasonable distraction because he didn't live in Dublin and was far away touring America.

I thought about him all the time, to get me through the nights at home. I thought about him when I cooked and when I bathed and when Ciaran had sex with me.

Then, he was headed back in our direction. He had gigs in Scotland and England, finishing with one in London, and asked me to come and see him.

I had been intentionally vague about what my situation was, saying only that I lived with my boyfriend but that things were complicated, implying perhaps that we were open, or had broken up already. I shouldn't have worried that he would care in any case. Part of what was between us was a conspiratorial acknowledgement that we were gross, that we were perverts, that it was nastiness bonding us together. He himself had some kind of long-term, on-again / off-again situation, which he would allude to occasionally without explanation or worry.

I knew as soon as he asked that I would go to see him, I could not imagine not doing it. There was money in my bank account and nothing to stop me. I foresaw in an instant the bus to the airport and the bad coffee on the plane and how excited I would feel pulling into the station. I booked a flight quickly before I could change my mind.

I told Ciaran that Lisa and Christina were going to see a gig and I was going to go with them. He was a little unhappy but not in any unmanageable sense, was trying to be cute about it.

'But I'll miss you,' he pouted. 'It's a long weekend; I thought we could hang out.'

I smiled and kissed him and booked a hotel.

It was the first time I had planned to cheat and the planning was almost as good as the doing, every boring bit of journey made potent. My alarm went off at five a.m. and I looked at his beautiful sleeping face and felt a pain so tender and engulfing it could hardly be called pain at all. I left and closed the door with the prickly knowledge that I was changing things.

I was doing something. I was finally doing something.

On the bus to the airport I did my make-up in exquisite, slow detail until I was completely beautiful.

When we arrived, two elderly women who had been sitting beside me grabbed my shoulder to tell me they'd been watching the whole time, amazed that I hadn't let my eyeliner or mascara slip, afraid I was going to poke my eye out! I was gorgeous, they said, and I was to enjoy my holidays. I smiled sweetly and went to find a bathroom to check my outfit.

On the train from Stansted to London I re-did my make-up and drank a quarter bottle of wine and brushed out my hair and took pictures of myself. I put one on Instagram and sent the same one to Ciaran.

Cute, he replied.

As the train pulled into Liverpool Street Station, light flooding down from the glass roof, I felt the incautious excitement I had as an eighteen-year-old moving to Dublin. That feeling of being young in a city, letting it do things to you, wanting to become something different in it.

It was lunchtime when I arrived at the hotel, a cheap one near London Bridge, and I took a long bath and removed all my make-up.

Noah and I messaged about how excited we were to see one another. My heart was pounding already, I couldn't stop smiling. I reminded myself not to start drinking until it was evening. We weren't meeting until eight p.m., at the bar in Brixton his band was playing.

At six I reapplied all my make-up and got dressed in a short blue dress I had bought specially, then went to the hotel bar and drank two gin and tonics on the patio.

A group of drunk German football fans were there too and cooed and shouted at me and I glared back with icy indifference. I looked so good. The discrepancy between what was going on inside me and how good I looked made this power of mine seem infinite.

The way that I looked lent all of the inward mess a saving grace, a chaotic glamour.

I will be glad for this when I'm old, I thought to myself, stubbing out another cigarette. I will want to remember this exact feeling, of sitting on a hotel patio waiting to go and have sex with a man I want so much I could faint.

I'll want to remember what it was like to have a body that couldn't be denied or regarded with ambivalence. I'll miss all of it, even the secrets, even the lies.

2

When I arrived at the bar he was standing smoking in the yard with the other guys from his band. He introduced me and they all smiled and said hello and didn't make me feel weird or smirk, although I imagine they all knew what I was there to do, that there could be no other reason for my presence.

They wandered back into the venue and he turned to me and framed my face with his rough hands and touched my hair, looking at me like he couldn't believe me – but not with seriousness, not in any earnest or embarrassing way, just like he was looking at a particularly interesting plant or animal or toy, something fun and pleasurable. He was simple and easy and so was the pleasure he took in me and the way I looked.

He led me over to his van, littered with guitars and empty fast-food containers, and we climbed into the front seat. We faced the shadow of an ivy-covered wall, but were exposed enough for it to feel absurd and dangerous. I sat straddling him and bent my neck to kiss him so that his head was submerged in the sweep of my hair. I thought distantly how clean I was compared to him. I smelled the hotel-fresh lavender shampoo on myself, and the weeks-old tobacco sweat of him.

I looked down at myself. I was white and pink and in a thin blue dress which squarely framed the tops of my breasts and ended halfway down my thighs. I was strawberry ice cream, blue sky. I smelled so good it was crazy.

He was sun-beaten, handsomely haggard from living out of a suitcase and off booze and burgers, his skin tawny and tough like a farmer's. He fumbled with his zip and his dick sprang loose; a stale, faintly urinary smell escaped with it and the distaste I felt made me more excited.

As in my dreams of fucking Freja, I could let myself feel pleasure from imagining it was me and not him who was doing the fucking.

I pushed myself into his head, tried to feel how it feels to crack something, someone, wide open.

I looked down at my body and was hysterical with the heat of invasion, mine and his.

He fucked me quickly and I let him come inside me, and walked back into the bar behind him, holding his hand, with the warm drool unfurling between my legs.

It felt like other men in the bar were looking at me appreciatively. I wondered if they could sense it somehow, if it was like being in heat, if they could smell his on me and wanted to cover it with their own.

Why does it take this to make me feel myself?

I was so myself, thinking of nobody but myself, I was nobody at all but myself in those moments.

2019, Athens

Sometimes, nowadays, when I am bored and alone, I try to speak to people. I talk to other lonely people in bars, I try to make them shocked enough to say something interesting, or to walk away from me.

If you saw me you would think I was very cruel, often laughing in the sad, soft faces of the kind of men who drink alone in this country, where drinking alone is not very normal, as they shrink away from me. They are grey-skinned, balding, spectacle-wearing. They are just the wrong side of gawky, wearing T-shirts of black metal bands and bad shorts, flirting hopelessly with the beautiful waitresses. They don't notice me so much any more. I am no longer a girl.

When I talk to them I ask, 'Do you think you are lovable?' And while they're thinking about it, or trying to turn away, I say quickly, 'Do you think it would be possible for anyone to love you if they could see every single thing you do?' And I watch them cringe as though I've reached out and struck them.

'I'm serious,' I say. 'Imagine that everyone could see everything. Every secret, every base physical ejection, every category of porn you've ever looked at in a kind of coma when you're numb to the normal stuff. Think about it all. Every moment of shame, of desperation – do you really think anyone could love you still? Anyone at all?'

3

I remember what it was like when I first loved Ciaran, before he left me that first time at Christmas, when I'd miss him so much when he went anywhere. He went to Limerick one long weekend to a conference and I had nothing to do with myself, nor did I want anything to do, I only wanted to be busy missing him.

I remember lying down in that lonely bedsit and thinking about him and crying. I wasn't crying because I was sad or worried, because I wasn't those things yet. And I wasn't crying because of the pain of missing him exactly. I was crying with a kind of enjoyment at the very fact that I *was* missing him, at that modest pain in me whenever I was missing a man.

It felt like a correct pain, a baseline state, and that was what was making me cry – how right and comforting. I could never be happy without him, but it was a nice pain, for it could be solved, I knew how to cure it.

And that's something to recommend love: that it has clear rules like a game, and it has speeches and sayings you'll have heard in films and in songs. There are patterns and there are steps to be taken. If you lose the game that's one thing, and that has to be dealt with, but at least there is a game to be played at all.

I remember when we were broken up I used to wake up crying, having dreamed all night that he was saying he loved me.

In the dream he was saying it and I was crying because I knew that he meant it.

I could feel it, I could almost taste the words, they were cool and delicious like a drink, but I knew that when I woke up it would stop being true.

I remember sitting watching him once when we were having a fight, or I was having one anyway.

He had kept commenting on what I was making us to eat, commenting on how much and what I was eating, until finally I asked him to stop, asked him why he did that all the time.

Immediately the shutter had gone down and his face closed up and he replied that my insecurities were my own problem and he couldn't be expected to rearrange everything for them. He couldn't watch what he said all the time just because I felt a certain way.

I cried when his face did that and said sorry and sorry and sorry but he was gone and moved away from me and sat by the window looking out and ignoring me.

He was lit up by the street lamps and the lights from the chipper across the road and even in my growing hysteria it still took me by surprise how beautiful he was in his absence, how like a painting or a statue sitting there like that. He could move so far away from me in a moment. I envied him his ability to remove himself.

He eked out his coldness a little at a time, for as long as we had known each other, while I saved all of mine for the end.

4

I remember that I read about Ian Tomlinson, a newspaper seller who died in the G20 protests in London in 2009 after being struck by a policeman. I was flipping through a newspaper and saw that he had died and found it sad. The next day there were more details, that he lived in a hostel, that he was an alcoholic, and that he had apparently said, 'I'm just trying to go home, I'm just trying to go home,' as he was dying. Reading that, I burst into tears in the passenger seat of my father's car. I imagined his life, his alcoholism, his life in that hostel, his just trying to go home. I cried for days.

When I was a young teenager I heard a story that, long before my time, in a rural village near Waterford, there was a woman who was poor and she sold sex to some of the village men, and that the wives of the village had made a plan and they had murdered her. They may not have meant to, but they did. They attacked her and put her on the ground and eventually she was dead.

Another story in a newspaper. A young church warden manipulated a decent, good man in his middle age who was a Christian. The Christian man was gay, and had never known how to reconcile his Christianity with that fact. The young church warden made the middle-aged man believe that they were in love, with a view to taking advantage of him and changing his will. He staged a ceremony to celebrate their relationship, after which he slowly poisoned the man until he believed that he was developing dementia. But not before making him think he had finally found love. 'At last I do not fear the prospect of dying alone,' the dying man wrote. You have to hope that he died before realising how alone he really was. You have to hope that he died still thinking that somebody loved him in the way he had wanted to be loved.

In our local paper when I was twelve: there was an elderly woman who would let some local kids hang around her house and she would make them cups of tea and give them biscuits, and of course that turned into some older kids bringing cans and smoking weed, and she didn't know how to make it stop and one day one of the older ones hurt her. When you hurt an old person their skin is paper thin – they made her whole face explode with blue and purple, and the look on her face was, *Why would they?* And why would they?

These stories hurt me so badly, but I've learned to react to that hurt by thinking of them again and again, forcing myself to replay the details over and over and over, until they are meaningless.

You grow cold, or you die yourself.

September 2014

1

Then there were others, in quick manic succession: first a friend, then a colleague, and finally an artist.

I was drinking more and more and Ciaran knew that I had changed. I was grovellingly sweet to him at certain high points, but then would disappear for whole nights and not apologise, just stumble in pissed and collapse on the bed.

I started to see my old friends again, and because years had passed and we were older now it was the really dedicated drunks who maintained the pace I had known before. There were only a few who could afford to keep it up, financially and physically. They were carefree and chronically depressed, artists and musicians with social capital who would be signing on the dole for the rest of their lives. They were the funniest people in Dublin, as long as you were drunk too.

They were still DJs and nightclub promoters, some of them, and the ones who had done well at that were able to justify their continued nightly excess. The rest of us justified it through them as a proxy – if we were going out, it was just to see our friends, and it so happened that our friends worked in bars that didn't open until eleven p.m. and necessitated great gulps of the cheap spirit-mixer on offer that week, and a not-inconsiderable number of trips to the bathroom to snort something or other off a key they held under your nose for you, politely.

I slept with the next man in this way, high and blind with drink, against the wall of a disabled toilet in a club on Harcourt Street. It was an old friend of mine called Mark who sold pills and played in four bands and who used to take me on hungover chaste dates to McDonald's when we knew each other years before.

I didn't remember the sex afterwards, not really, only the sniggering friends of his looking over at us from behind the DJ booth after we left the toilet, and me stumbling home along the canal by myself afterwards.

2

I was talking to Noah all this time. He was unreal – or what he meant to me was unreal – but he seemed like a miracle, bursting off my screen whenever he contacted me, his cleverness and weird hilarity. I would walk around all day and not look up at all. He took pictures of what he was eating and what he was seeing and told me what he was thinking without me asking him to.

After the freeze of Ciaran, Noah's warmth was stunning, a sensory overload, a person without barrier. The idea that one could live that way was so wonderful, I didn't know whether to believe it or not. Was it just a choice?

What was good about him was that he wasn't even the most important part of what made him good. He made the world itself seem good and ripe and ready to be run towards, he made me feel funny and new and fizzing, and like he wouldn't even need to be there for that to be true.

3

I received an email from Lisa, still happy in Berlin with her girlfriend and new unknowable life.

Though we hardly knew the business of each other's lives any more, I knew we still loved each other. She told me in her email that she was finishing the first draft of her book.

I swallowed, throat prickly with pride and envy – my one dream in childhood was to make a book.

When I was small, before drinking and men and the rest, books were the thing that could absorb me entirely and let me forget myself.

I had liked the idea of making something for someone else to do that in. It seemed like the only thing I might have a real desire to do.

That was a long time ago, of course, and now it seemed borderline incomprehensible to me that someone could dedicate so much time and effort to a thing without a known outcome.

Life was so pointless, so opaque and shifting, that I could only think about immediate feelings.

Immediacy was all I had.

4

Then it was the same ugly obnoxious colleague who had groped me at the office party, on another night out – the one who had affected me so deeply by asking how Ciaran could have let me out like that.

Another blurred, weeping memory of him, of my initial drunken and reluctant compliance.

Then eventually something like enjoyment or at least need, a need to have his repellent hands all over me, I remember crying with his hands on my throat, the awful smell of his rotten inside self, the way he made me feel more Ciaran's and more myself all at once, how powerful that was, how terrible.

5

And finally, there was an artist Ciaran shared a studio with, a sickly-looking pretty young student with a fashionably horrible haircut.

I turned up there one Saturday night, their fourth-floor room on the quays, after having been out drinking and dancing until two. I went to see if Ciaran was around, my phone, as ever, having died in the early evening. I had forgotten about this boy, who was young and shy and unmemorable.

When I knocked on the door he opened it with his pained, timid expression and told me that Ciaran had left hours before. He offered me a beer and we sat on the desks where I'd seen Ciaran work, and we talked and drank until he was drunk too, and then we kissed and then we had sex.

He alternated between seeming frightened and being erratically violent, hitting me and pinching me in the softest places and then shrinking back into himself.

I felt sorry afterwards, not just for myself this time, but for the boy too, for making him a part of anything.

I felt sorry for whatever was wrong inside him, whatever made him lash out and withdraw, lash out and withdraw.

6

I woke up in the morning on my own, the light from the long studio windows burning all over me and my dry mouth gasping.

I was naked and covered with a piece of tarpaulin. I gathered it to my body and propped myself up, shading my eyes and squinting out at that grand grey light over the Liffey you get on cold early mornings.

It was the first day of November in Dublin and it was my birthday. I was twenty-five years old.

My stomach was roiling, awash with acid. My lip was cut and swollen from being hit. My knees and the insides of my thighs were bruised, between my legs bloody, and inside of me there was semen eking out.

I was alone.

I crawled along the floor with one hand on my throbbing head to find my bag and fumble for my phone, plugged it in and lay heavily down beside it.

I pressed my hot bruised face against the wall, which smelled of paint and reminded me of school.

(And I thought then of how it had been once there, in school, how much I loved Bea and how we swapped notes all day long. We struggled not to convulse with laughter, vibrating and becoming purple with it, sometimes exploding helplessly at the doodles and nicknames and nonsense and getting hauled out by a teacher. Remembered going home one midterm and literally praying to God that we wouldn't be moved from sitting next to each other in the classroom, as had been threatened many times, because I loved her so much.)

The wall felt cold and soothing against the parts of my face that were swollen and tender, places the strange, sad boy had struck me without warning.

I wondered how they always knew that I was someone to be hurt.

Even when I didn't tell them to, they knew somehow that there was a part of me that accepted or desired it.

But how was it that they knew?

Why was it that nobody ever thought to ask me in which way I wanted to be hurt, or for how long, or how hard?

And if they had asked, would I have known what to tell them?

I turned on my phone.

There were dozens of missed calls from Ciaran which I scrolled through blankly, and there were messages from Noah, messages teasing and being rude and telling me what he was up to, and saying he missed me.

Noah.

To think of him was fortifying in the wreckage of that morning. He was sturdy and strong and happy. He made me laugh and feel it was possible for things to start over.

He was smart without being boring, he talked in such a way as to make me think of new things, things I'd never thought of on my own.

He knew what he wanted to do in the world, and he made himself happy by enjoying it. I wanted to be near him, to absorb his surety.

I wanted him to touch me gently sometimes and harshly at others, and for us both always to know, without asking, which one was right in that moment.

I thought of his sleepy eyes fondly regarding me, like I was a thing of value he coveted and knew that he deserved, his lazy smile and the irreducible him-ness of him. To know him even a little bit was to sense the fullness of his character, how it burst through his every joke and kiss and exclamation.

There was so much him to grapple with, what was in him was so crowded and chaotic and vibrant that it felt like I would never get bored of sorting through it. With him it felt that there was no shortage of world to discuss, that there were no blank spaces or full stops.

The thought of him filled me up comfortingly, reduced the scratchiness in my worn-out smoky throat and the tenderness of the bruising. Lessened the adrenalin and fear from the terrible hangover. If I could just stay in a single moment with him, talking to him and making him smile down at his phone as I was doing now.

In his messages he said that he was going to move to London for at least a few months in January, recording with a band there and seeing how things went, and did I want to come and stay for a while?

Did I?

I saw it, felt it, straight away.

The journey to the airport, having hastily packed up my things in the apartment while Ciaran shouted at me.

The unbeatable feeling of being young and alone and on your way to the next thing.

The cold clear air, moving fast on the icy tarmac towards the terminals, the sheer pleasure of meeting Noah there and being so free of everything I had done to myself.

The pleasure of simply seeing what would happen.

We could talk about it all, and about Ciaran, how wrong I had been to choose a person like that, how painful it was to try to love someone for so long. He would reassure me that things would be better now and let me cry sometimes

255

and then we would fuck and be happy and live together in this new place, brand new to each other.

On Sundays we would go to Deptford and New Cross where his friends lived and roast chickens and drink the five-pound fizz from Sainsbury's.

I would work in cafés or pubs and write in the daytimes while Noah was busy, and in the mornings take long walks around the Rye in Peckham or all the way to London Bridge and then go along the river.

I would go to Broadway Market with him and eat samples of all the best things and buy some stinky olives to walk around with. We wouldn't have anything to do. The walking around would be the point.

And when he played gigs I would go to some of them – not all, because I would have my own life, too – and look at him performing and feel proud and turned on by the privacy of the public act, his face contorting and breaking into curious ecstatic smiles at high points.

It wouldn't be just us in the world because he wasn't that sort of person, couldn't be contained even if I wanted to do that to him. I would love him because of his expansiveness, his open heart and greedy appetites. I wouldn't want to contain him.

Some weekends we would get the train to Kent and take day-long walks, stomping over the coastline for fifteen miles.

(But that wouldn't be like you, Ciaran would say if he heard. Hiking? And that would be the point – it wouldn't be me at all any more.)

Or maybe it would be different to that. Maybe it would be a kind of life I couldn't even imagine. Something I had no grounding in, something without precedent.

I let myself think of all this for a few moments and feel the relief it would bring.

To let an entirely new thing take me over, which was the only way I would escape Ciaran alive, that woozy joy of being able to leave a whole life, my whole self, behind me in an instant.

But I didn't know him.

But he was just another image.

But I wouldn't be young and alone – I would be young and on my way to someone else.

Noah was as different to Ciaran as could be, it was true, but I hadn't changed.

I would still be the same, I knew, no matter how badly I would have liked to believe otherwise.

It might feel at first like I was leaving, swept up in a new, never-felt-before euphoria, but one day soon that theory would crumble (and probably not very long afterwards – Noah's drinking problem mirroring my own, his rarely spoken-of possible-girlfriend, his natural need to flirt with everyone he met).

I would be leaving in desperation, not joy, would be bolting away from something as much as towards another.

No, there would be no end to it that way. There would be no end to it unless I made one myself.

7

I got straight into a taxi from the studio, not wanting to leave time enough to tidy myself up and have the chance to change my mind. I can't remember ever having adrenalin like that, every last inch of me jittering and bumping off the other parts and my heart moving frighteningly from the alcohol and the knowledge of what I was going to do.

Two parts of me were panicking for different reasons.

The standard part, the one that depended on the daily-ness of Ciaran and the promise of never being left alone, was trying to stop me, trying to tell me how to cover for this one, to clean myself up and lie.

And now there was another part, and it was so strong and fast it seemed to be powering the speeding taxi through force of will, a part telling me to run, run, run. To get out as quickly and as completely as I could. To burn down the house, to lock him inside, to forget it all as rapidly as reality would allow.

The daily part tried to soothe me, tried running a quick show reel of the good times Ciaran and I had shared, the ones which mitigated all the rest. And I did see them, the relief of getting into a quiet bed with him of an evening, the relief of his occasional dazzling good moods and the way he could be amusing then, the relief of him taking care of me when I was ill.

I thought then that that was all those times were: relief. They were always relief from the absence of what I feared, the ordinary, truly daily things: the coldness, and the ignorance, and the disdain, and the hatred.

The chiding and the shaping of me, the backhanded compliments and barbed advice. The constant knowledge that I would never, ever be what he wanted. The pleasure wasn't often pleasure; it was release from pain. It was binding yourself and feeling good when the bandages came off, it was cutting a hole in your leg so you could feel it heal.

I had suffered, and I had made the suffering into something I could consider good. I made it so that suffering was a kind of work.

8

I stumbled out of the taxi, on to Rathmines Road, and it was early enough that a gang of thirty-somethings laughed at me in my state, perhaps amiably recognising their past selves in me.

I put my key in the door of our flat but before I could turn it, it swung open.

He looked at me, up and down, and then turned away and took the stairs two at a time. I followed behind, heart going like anything in my throat. I walked into our living room. I put my bag and my things down on the table, and collapsed heavily on to our couch.

'I want to break up,' I said.

My head was still swimmingly drunk.

'Oh, really?' he said mockingly.

He wasn't surprised. I felt a sudden relief. Maybe it would be so easy. Maybe he had known it was coming. Maybe he felt the same way!

'Why do you want to break up?' he asked, eyes still doing the cold sarcastic dance.

I didn't know how to respond. I had expected the statement to be its own event, had expected him to be angry and shocked and shouting.

He turned then, towards our bedroom, and indicated with a brief wave that I should follow him.

He moved swiftly and smoothly as ever.

I stumbled along the corridor grasping at the walls, head now starting to really thump.

I turned into our room, where he sat on the edge of the bed.

All around him were my diaries.

He had arranged them so that they fanned extravagantly, taking up the entire space.

The words were all there. What I had done. Who I had fucked.

The things I felt about Noah.

My frustration and eventual boredom with him, Ciaran.

He sat in the middle of it all, grinning a terrible slow, hot grin and turned to one of the notebooks and read it aloud to me.

'I don't know why I am the way that I am. I don't know why I need to be knocked around and hurt and humiliated in the way that I do. I have no insight into my reasons. But it simply is true that I do want those things and that Ciaran does not seem to have any interest in giving them to me.'

He looked up at me again with that awful smile leaking into his usually beautiful face.

'I'm sorry,' I said, and it was almost comic because it was so inadequate.

I was shaking. I needed sugar, cold water, a shower. I needed to leave.

'I'm sorry,' I said again.

And it sounded so thin even I didn't believe it, but then I began to cry. I sat down in the corner and put my head in my lap and wept and wept. With one hand I hid my face, and with the other I grasped for him. I touched his hand and then he stood up.

'You didn't tell me you wanted that,' he said.

I was crying still, not registering what he was saying, or what he was doing.

He was unbuckling his belt. He was undoing his button and his zip. I was curled into the furthest reach of the bedroom, hiding myself from what was going on, from my shame. I was holding a T-shirt of his to my face to catch the tears and to breathe into.

He was undressed then.

He kneeled where I was and kissed me and the feeling of him not hating me was so good and so unexpected. I kissed him back, ecstatic with relief.

Then he pushed his hands up my dress quickly and roughly. I made a noise of surprise.

He kissed me more, gently. I felt absolved for a moment. He was forgiving me.

He grabbed at my underwear violently, dragging it off me and up-ending me in the process.

'Hey!' I murmured, surprised out of my crying, upset, for the first time, by the strangeness of the situation and by his behaviour.

He pressed his hand down on my lower abdomen just above my crotch, to keep me still. My heart was beating so fast. His touching me was making me feel so sick but it felt necessary. I thought to myself, *If it's just this, and then I can go, I can do that.*

He started fucking me and I closed my eyes and rolled them backward, trying to get the white light and sparks. Then he hit me.

He slapped me first, and when I didn't open my eyes, he hit me with his fist. I looked up at him, mouth open, shocked.

'I thought this is what you like?' he said.

I began to cry, and to squirm.

When I squirmed enough that he couldn't comfortably fuck me any more, he dragged me up by my hair. He put his dick in my mouth while he forced me from behind my neck, and fucked me that way.

262

I began to cry, really cry.

'Stop crying, you bitch,' he said, and I looked up at him then, through my tears, and I saw that he hated me. He hated me entirely and completely.

'I thought you liked this,' he said again as he fucked my throat. And when I cried more, he sneered down at me.

'This is what you like,' he kept saying.

9

When he had finished he walked straight into the shower.
I packed a bag quickly and left.
I stayed in a hotel that night, soaking in a scalding bath.
Two weeks later I left the country.

May 2015
Athens

1

After Ciaran and I broke up, and I had been in Greece for six months, my friend Mark asked to visit. I had been alone a long time by then and my loneliness was of a different nature to what it had been both before and during my relationship with Ciaran. It existed in a more permanent and peaceful way, felt like a thing that could reasonably be expected to be endured for ever. I could not tell yet whether this feeling was one I should resist.

My new aversion to company felt perverse and dangerous somehow, implied ensuing decades of strange behaviour, suggested a finality I was not sure I wanted.

One day I realised I had not spoken to any person for a week. On the metro a man with a moustache and strong tan arms wrapped his hand around the pole I was leaning on, and I had to stop myself leaning forward just an inch to brush my cheek against its smooth brown back.

2

Mark arrived. It felt wrong to be speaking with another person, and one I could barely remember knowing. My words were hesitant, and getting drunk, which I had not done in weeks, did not help. When I told him how I was spending time – working, walking, reading, writing – it sounded lethargic and relaxing instead of how it felt, which was constantly charged with the newness of loss, the shock of chaos.

He kept saying how amazing I was, how brilliant my work must be, how great I looked, how special a person I was.

When, in conversation, I referred to having a bad day and not being able to work well, he immediately denied that such a thing was possible.

I hate now for men to dote in this way, the ones who don't know me. Their praise lands uncertainly in the air somewhere between the two of us, because it doesn't belong to me. I hate to hear them tell me what I am, even or especially when what they think I am is kind or brilliant or beautiful. I hate when they insist that I have no faults, that my laziness or violence or cruelty simply don't exist.

When they speak this way I am even less in my body than usual, feeling the sickness of a stranger look me in the eye and describe what is not there. What I am feeling is their disregard for my reality. I am being made to wear whatever particular fantasy they wish to project.

Each time it happens I have to restrain myself from screaming in their faces to prove I am not what they believe me to be. In these moments I am happy with my ugliness and want them to see it. Whatever badness I am I want to be it, to be as much like whatever my self is as possible; as far from the stranger's projection as possible.

'I think it's just great,' he kept saying, in response to any inanity I told him about what I had been up to. 'Coming here all alone, it's so brave.'

I restrained myself from snapping in disagreement. What was brave about it? I was where I was because I was too stupid and weak to be with other people. I had needed them too much and had been destroyed by it. Now I was too afraid to try such a thing again, having got the whole idea so catastrophically wrong, and so instead I was here.

I was also here because I could be. I was lucky enough to be able to run. I had no money, but also no dependents. I was young and agile and had no responsibilities that could not be shed in a matter of weeks.

There was nothing brave about it. I had been braver every night I spent locked in the bathroom after a fight with Ciaran. I was braver every day I got up the next morning and went to work. Who would ever understand this, that the weakness was also steely and pure? In a way I myself could no longer understand.

I hate my weakness, what I severed of myself and gave to him, but love it too, love it still. I do not take it back. I love the girl who did those things. I love the girl because I feel sorry for her, and understand her.

Is it brave to be alone? Maybe, in a way. But it was also brave to ask someone to be with me, even though it was the wrong person, and in the wrong way. How could I have asked him to love me, day after day, when the answer kept on being no? What desperation made me live that way?

I mourn for that braveness, which is gone; whether it's gone for ever or not, I don't yet know.

That night Mark kissed me and I let him. It was the easy thing to do, the only thing to do. The idea of telling him not to and the ensuing conversation filled me with weariness. I wondered how many times in my life I had made this calculation, how the men would feel if they knew, if they would care.

In my bedroom, his fawning was irritating me so much that at first kissing was a relief. Then he kept stopping to draw back and look at my face and do this move of slightly shaking his head in – what? – wonder? And then smiling and returning to kiss again. Every time he did it I felt worse and worse, more and more desperate for it to end. Sometimes he would laugh a little, as though in disbelief at his good fortune. It all felt rehearsed.

After it had gone on a while, I pushed away and said I was going to brush my teeth and get into my pyjamas. I hoped this would be enough to neutralise the intimation that sex was to follow. I hoped that we could just go to sleep.

When I returned, I shut off the light and climbed into bed with my back to him, with an overly cheery and definitive, 'Goodnight!' Behind me, shirtless, he inched nearer and then pressed his body into mine and thrust his arm around my front. He started to slowly stroke my ribs, his mouth was moving through my hair towards my neck. He kissed me there, my ears, was whispering some endearment. I stayed still and hoped this would be enough, that he would give up. He took my jaw in his hand and jerked it back to face him, began to kiss me. I kissed him back.

After his hands had run over my breasts and he was edging underneath my T-shirt I put my hand on his wrist.

270

'I'm tired, I don't feel like it. I'm sorry,' I said. He lay on his back. I looked at him: his eyes were wide and pleading. I turned back around and put my arm over my head, gathering the blanket to me.

A few minutes later his body had moved back to cradle mine. I ignored it. *I can sleep like this*, I thought, *I can deal with this*. His dick got hard and he began, gently at first and then less so, to push it into me. His face was again rustling in my hair and softly kissing me.

'I don't want to,' I forced myself to say, instead of doing what I was inclined to – rolling over, giving in. I wondered if he knew how unbearable it was for me to say this to him, if he knew how every cell in my body was inclined to yield.

'Aw, why not?' he replied in the tone of a kid told he was no longer allowed to play video games.

How could I answer this?

Why not you now, Mark, when there have been so many others, and indeed you yourself have been one?

Why did I want it before and not now?

Why do your little laughs and smiles nauseate me?

It's not that my body means any more to me now than it once did, it's only that I hate you more.

I resent the fact that you can take pleasure from me.

The comedian John Belushi once said, 'I give so much pleasure to so many people. Why can't I get some pleasure for myself?'

I don't think you deserve it. Don't think you deserve me.

I think your little pantomime of friendship and desire is weak and pallid.

He kept on kissing my neck, tenderly stroking my body. I kept myself turned stiffly away. My eyes were wide open and staring blankly ahead.

'Why not?' he said again, and as I turned towards him I saw he was grinning at me. He was actually grinning, sheepish and happy. He kept touching me and eventually

I did what I had to do to stop him from wanting to have sex with me, which was to have sex with him.

I made loud low noises which only an idiot would mistake for noises of animalistic pleasure. I focused on making these noises, which were letting out some of the hatred and revulsion inside me. As he went faster and started to hurt me I leaned backwards and scratched his thighs as hard as I could.

Again, an idiot might mistake this for a sign of abandonment, enjoyment. His little whimpers disgusted me.

I looked at the ceiling, willing him to finish, hot frustrated tears gathering in my eyes. I moved my body up and down faster and faster, begging him in my head to finish, finish, finish. When he did I rolled away from him and thought to myself never again never again never again.

I give so much pleasure to so many people. Why can't I get some pleasure for myself?

I thought, not for the first time, that wheedling of the sort he had employed should be forbidden in men. It was already so near to impossible to say no to a man, so difficult to accept the possibility of being hurt or disliked or shouted at. It takes so much out of you to make yourself say no when you have been taught to say yes, to be accommodating, to make men happy.

Once you've said no, a man wheedling feels unbearable. Even if he does it politely, or gently, it overrides the clearly expressed intention. It says: Your choice does not really matter. What I desire matters, and I don't want to feel bad for forcing you into it. So perhaps you ought to reconsider?

Wheedling is cowardly, and violent. When you change someone's no to yes by wheedling, you have stolen from them what does not belong to you.

It was the last thing I wanted to do, and I did it.

I sat up beside him in bed, looking at my thighs. As usual my body looked different to me after somebody had fucked it, more coherent than before. He put his arm around me and chattered about his job, his bands, telling stories, staff gossip. He was easier to listen to now, less grating. I was able to laugh along without it hurting too much.

3

When I sleep with men I don't like, men who irritate or scare or disgust me, because it is easier to do so, I make myself as bad as they are. I drag myself down to their level by allowing them to have what they want.

Having sex with them degrades me, my reluctance and eventual capitulation degrade me. Once I have been degraded I am really no better than they are. The men themselves are rendered more bearable to me.

I hate them less afterwards, because I've made myself as pathetic as they are.

4

I woke early on Sunday morning and went to the balcony to check my emails and smoke. It was a beautiful day.

Athens had already given me this gift: I appreciated every day that I existed there. It made me more happy to be alive than not. The idea of not living was absurd. You would be mad to not live as long as you can in Greece.

I'd like to swim today, I thought.

When Mark woke up I hustled him out of the apartment quick as I could so we wouldn't miss the warmer part of the afternoon. The nearest beach was an hour away and I made sure to check he had brought a book before we left.

We sat in companionable silence on the tram journey, I felt sorry for him that I hated him so much.

As I undressed on the beach he told me he couldn't really swim very well; he was fine to a certain point but didn't like to go in very far.

'Fine, that's OK, don't worry,' I said brusquely, not caring what he was or wasn't able to do.

I walked and then swam into the cold ocean, turned on my back and looked at the sky, stretched out my limbs a bit below the surface before going too far.

I was happy, as I always am in the sea, the only place I have ever found where my body feels natural and mine and being used according to its intent. I am weightless but not insubstantial. I am always sure of what my body should be doing there. I feel seal-like, the fat I normally hate becomes sleek and normal in water, my inelegant body can be strong there.

Mark waded in, gasping and wincing at the cold. He grinned at me, teeth chattering, edging his way towards me. It took him a minute to work himself up to submersion. Then he paddled towards me and grabbed me by the waist, manoeuvring my body to try to have my legs wrapped around his torso. I submitted to the pose for a few moments and let him kiss me, then bent backwards and kicked away.

After I got a little further out I glanced back at him.

Seeing him there, squirming in the tide, unsure and uncomfortable, I understood fully that certain weaknesses in others are intolerable – at least they are when you don't love them.

I remembered how Ciaran would want me to do certain things that I couldn't or was not willing to, physical things like cycling or running. I would decline and apologise for my shortcomings, shortcomings that were as certainly and definitively me as my own face was.

You don't mind, do you? I would say, an ironic pout, trying to be playful, acknowledging my own limitations; I fully expected him to love me in spite of them.

Of course I don't mind, he would say, and I would mostly believe him. But there was always a hint of the unsaid in these conversations, a harsh word he didn't let out, a bit of distaste.

I understood it, looking at Mark. Someone who needs you, even just a little – who needs you to like or love them – seeing their weakness is disturbing and repellent. It's ugly but it's true.

It isn't fair, but there it is. When you love a person these things are nothing, or even lovable in and of themselves. But when you don't love a person, they niggle at you. The person's humanity is revealed too soon, before you can come to forgive it with love.

I knew then that Ciaran had not loved me. At least he didn't love me in a right way, a way that had to do with who I was.

It didn't make it good, what I had done to him, what we had done to each other. But it made it OK. It made it something I could live with.

I swam as far out as I could without stopping to breathe, and then came up, far from shore, so far I could not see the expression on anyone's face, so far that I could not be kept track of. I was happy he couldn't follow me, and kept going. I swam until I was exhausted, my arms and legs getting so jellied that I struggled to return, the hotels and umbrellas and people all blurring happily.

When I got back to the shore, Mark was sitting up on the towel, reading a book, ill-concealed annoyance on his face.

'I couldn't see you any more ... I was worried,' he said.

I collapsed down into the sand, stretching myself into it and wriggling around, letting it get into all the awkward parts of myself.

'That's OK,' I said to him. 'There's no need.'

5

He left then, taking the keys to the apartment.

Near me two elderly twin brothers were sunbathing and moving in sync on their towels to tan evenly. They stood up together and faced the last bit of afternoon light with their eyes closed and holding hands, not speaking.

It made me happy, how funny and touching they were, and how comfortable with one another.

It made me happy too to look around me at the hot dog stand and at my beer set down in the sand, and my sour Greek cigarettes, and the books I had bought earlier that week from a woman's porch.

It made me so happy that soon I was crying at the luck I'd had in getting here, how lucky I was to be on my own at last, even when it hurt.

There were things happening inside me which there were no words for, or too many words – things that were so simple that they seemed infantile to even think of but which I hadn't been able to think of for so long. Things like the creamy orange sky which was making my heart feel split and open and free as it had when I was a teenager.

I remembered how much I had once loved to learn things. I could see myself back in the library in Waterford surrounded by reference books and encyclopedias, where I would sit all day, learning things because I wanted to know them, not to tell them to anybody else or to become someone different than I really was.

I thought of Mark's annoyed face and his worry for me when he could no longer keep track of me snaking off into the ocean, where I floated on my back and enjoyed the smell of my perfume coming off the water.

I thought of all the worry I had solicited in one way or another from Ciaran and from other men, with the food and the cutting and the crying and the sex, the whole great presentation of my rage and hurt, anger like a performance, anger at everything they'd done to me or hadn't bothered doing to me.

I thought how full my life and my head had been for ever with these things, with the desperation to be loved by a man, with the idea that a man's adoration or need to fuck me would make all the bad parts of myself be quiet for ever.

I'd thought that a man's love would make me so full up I'd never need to drink or eat or cut or do anything at all to my body ever again. I'd thought they'd take it over for me.

But now here I was, right inside it, with nobody to say what happened next.

What would I think about, now that I wasn't thinking about love or sex? That would be the next thing, trying to figure out what to fill up all that space with.

But that was all right. That would follow.

CAVAN COUNTY LIBRARY

Acknowledgements

To my remarkable, brilliant and beloved agent and friend Harriet Moore: I wouldn't have written this book without you and will forever be grateful for your unflagging faith in this awkward, changeable work in all its various forms. You are so loved and so admired by me and many others.

I am very grateful for the incredible guidance and unswerving vision given to me so generously and kindly by Jonathan Cape, especially Michal Shavit and Ana Fletcher, and at Little Brown from the inimitable Jean Garnett.

Thank you to the friends who supported me while I wrote this book, whether through lent fifty quids, roast dinners or just the relief of their entertainment and company. Thanks to my beloved Taddyheads: Stan Cross, Francisco Garcia, Josh Baines and Charles Olafare, to my Pink IPA gals Lolly Adefope, Heather McIntosh and Thea Everett for chatting to me all day every day and making me crease constantly. To Crispin Best, Mat Riviere and Rachel Benson for being such good friends when I first arrived to London and forever more: I love you all and treasure each time we're together.

Thanks to everyone who provided me with short term house and cat sitting opportunities where I got chunks of writing done in often very delightful surroundings, especially Tommy and Kate Farrell and Sophie Jung.

Thank you to Jesse Darling for being a brief but excellent and formative London housemate and providing a much needed idea of what a positive rather than sacrificial domesticity might be like.

Joseph Noonan Ganley, Fiona Byrne, Chris Timms, Frank Wasser and Alice Rekab for hospitality and invitations when I first arrived to London and baked potatoes and Christmas parties in Camberwell, and willingness to discuss work when it was in embryonic embarrassing stages.

Lovely Linda Stupart and Tom, I admire both of you kind, brilliant people so much and am inspired by your love for each other. Let's go back to Ischia.

Thanks to Roy Claire Potter my favourite chain-smoking, chain-everything pal and one of the best writers and artists I've ever come across.

Thanks to my former housemate and wonderful friend Isadora Epstein for our years in Dublin laughing and discussing and for all your support when I was there and since I left- you're the absolute tops lady. Thanks to Oisin Murphy Hall and Liz Ni Mhairtin for the years of friendship, for putting me up when I'm back in Dublin and for making me laugh like nobody else can. Thanks to my dear friend Fiona Hallinan for thirteen years of friendship, fish, swims – you are a wonder. To Shane Morrissey, my most cherished bully.

To Sean Goucher, forever my favourite former colleague.

Thank you to my fantastic brothers Gavan and Luke Flinter for your support and love and the always entertaining and often whiskey-soaked Christmastime rumbles.

To Simon Childs: thank you for your easy and generous love which made the writing of this opposite kind of love much more bearable. You will always be close to my heart and I hope we will know each other for the rest of our lives.

To my best friend Doireann Larkin: I love you so much and can't say how forever grateful I will be for all your help when I came to London – giving me Oyster cards and dinners in Tupperware and wine when I was hard up, and all the silly never ending nights on your couch telling each other the same stories as we have been for fifteen years and enjoying them just as much as ever.

Thank you to my wonderful step parents, Ger Kenny and Trudi Hartley.

Most of all thank you to my parents Jim Nolan and Sue Larkin for sticking by me while I blew my life into bits over and over and while I put it back together again. Without your patience, love and encouragement I wouldn't have made it out the other side. Thank you so much, I love you so much.

MEGAN NOLAN

Megan Nolan lives in London and was born in 1990 in Waterford, Ireland. Her essays, fiction and reviews have been published in the *New York Times*, *White Review*, *Sunday Times*, *Village Voice*, *Guardian* and in the literary anthology, *Winter Papers*. She writes a fortnightly column for the *New Statesman*. This is her first novel.